3 1336 00044 4753

D0971548

THE GOLDEN OYSTER

Also by Donald Gordon:

STAR-RAKER

THE FLIGHT OF THE BAT

THE GOLDEN OYSTER

By DONALD GORDON

William Morrow & Company, Inc.

NEW YORK, 1968

Second Printing, January 1969

An abridged version of this novel was published in Great Britain in serial form in December 1967-January 1968 issues of *Woman's Own*.

Printed in the United States of America.

Library of Congress Catalog Card Number 68-18584

Author's Note

THE Rommel treasure is no figment of the imagination. It exists: about £6,000,000 of bullion, jewels and paper currency sunk during the war off the coast of Africa. The ship in which it was being carried is known to have gone down in deep water five or six miles off a certain Libyan port; but all efforts to find the treasure have failed.

In the spring of 1963 I took part, with my friend Edwin Link, in an attempt to locate the treasure. We made use of what were then the very latest techniques of deep-sea diving—as reported in the *New Scientist* and the *National Geographic*—and *The Golden Oyster* is partly based on our experiences.

I have, for obvious reasons, altered the location; and the characters are fictitious. But the story of the Rommel treasure is firmly rooted in fact, and the background of deep-sea diving is authentic.

D.G.

Author's Note

THE Rommel treasure is no figment of the imagination. It exists: about [illegible] of bullion, jewels and paper currency sunk during the war off the coast of Corsica. The ship in which it was being carried is known to have gone down in deep water five or six miles off a certain Corsican port; but all efforts to find the treasure have failed.

In the spring of [illegible] I took part, with my friend Edwin Link, in an attempt to locate the treasure. We made use of what were then the very latest techniques of deep sea diving—as reported in the *New Yorker* and the *National Geographic*—and *The [illegible]* is partly based on our experiences.

I have, for obvious reasons, altered the location; and the characters are fictions. But the story of the Rommel treasure is firmly rooted in fact, and the background of deep sea diving is authentic.

[illegible]

PROLOGUE

It all started with the letter. His apprenticeship to violence, his falling in love (at an age when he thought he was past such frivolity), the acquisition of wealth beyond his wildest dreams: they all stemmed from the little azure envelope which the postman pushed through the letter box of Dragonfly Cottage one afternoon in late September.

Peter Grey, the most junior of the many partners of Blake, Son and Sturman, Solicitors, noticed the envelope as soon as he arrived home from the office. The green ink and the neat, backward-sloping handwriting almost rang a bell: almost but not quite: and he slipped the letter into his pocket and got on with helping to bathe the children—a job which had become daily routine since the death of his wife. He didn't get round to opening the letter until he and his elder daughter were finishing their supper; then, pushing aside his plums and custard, he slit open the envelope casually and without any sort of premonition that here was something which would alter the course of his life. The letter was short:

My dear Peter,

The bread that many years ago you cast on the waters can now be returned; and if the idea of becoming a millionaire appeals to you then I suggest we meet at Lob's Wood Hotel, Tilford, at about six-thirty p.m. tomorrow (Tuesday). It is quiet there and we can reminisce about the good old days in general and the night we were taken prisoner in particular.

My love to Jean and the family,

Ken Richards

Being a solicitor, Peter Grey was not given to precipitate judgments. He read the letter twice, then handed it without comment to his daughter.

She made a little gesture of bewilderment: "Who on earth's Ken Richards?"

"The Fleet Air Arm observer I flew with in the war."

"Yes, of course. Is this," she smoothed out the folds in the letter, "some sort of joke?"

"Ken Richards," her father said slowly, "was always a bit of a wild one. But I wouldn't have thought this was *meant* as a joke."

"He says he wants to reminisce about the night you were taken prisoner." Her voice was puzzled. "What happened?"

"Among other things Ken saved my life. But it was all a very long time ago!"

She sensed his mood with clinical precision: his faintly guilty nostalgia for the exciting times that would never come again, his feeling that the years were slipping aimlessly by. She loaded the remains of their supper on to a tray. "Enjoy your coffee," she said. "I'll do the washing up."

He was grateful, but he insisted on helping her. He felt that for an attractive young girl of seventeen she spent too much of her life at the kitchen sink.

By the time they had finished their chores it was dark and cool, with mist forming white in the knees of the hills. They hadn't discussed the letter while they were washing up; but it had been on their minds: enigmatic, tantalizing, and with a connotation of danger and adventure to which they were strangers. When the last of the plates was stacked, Peter Grey tossed a couple of logs on the sitting-room fire: "You going out tonight?"

She gestured to the grand piano which took up almost a third of the sitting room: "I *ought* to practice. But I'd much rather hear what happened to you and this Ken Richards."

He walked to the window and drew back the curtains. He didn't often talk to his children about the war; but Anne, he reminded himself, was no longer a child, and having shown her the letter he owed her an explanation. He hesitated. It was the moon that finally tipped the scales: the enormous blood-red moon suspended over the fields at the back of the cottage. It brought back memories: memories of the night, twenty-five years ago, when in the light of just such a moon his Swordfish had toppled flaming into the Gulf of Sidra. "It's hard," he said slowly, "to know just where to begin."

She curled catlike on a cushion in front of the fire. "Then begin at the beginning. Tell me everything that happened that night the two of you were taken prisoner."

The dunes and escarpments, he told her, glowed like phosphorous in the light of the moon. Over Egypt the sky was clear, but over the Gulf of Sidra storm clouds were massing darkly. The date was 27th August, 1942: the time a shade after midnight: the place Royal Naval Air Station Ma'aten Bagush on the fringe of the Libyan desert.

A Tannoy blared raucously into the night—"Sub-lieutenants Richards and Grey, Cridland and Strong report to briefing." The airfield stirred reluctantly to life; lights flickered and were quickly doused, a pair of Mark II Swordfish were towed on to the hard-standing, and a flare truck nosed round the perimeter track and on to the duty runway.

It was hot and airless as a few minutes later the pilots and observers made their way from tents to crew room. Their shadows, in the light of a haloed moon, moved ghostlike over the airfield, and dust kicked up by their sandals hung motionless in the air a long time after they had passed. Ken Richards peered at the moon without enthusiasm: "Looks like we're in for a storm."

"Come on then"—Peter Grey pulled open the door of the crew room— "the sooner we're off, the sooner we'll be back."

But in this he turned out to be wrong.

The moment the four of them stepped into the roomful of senior officers they could sense the tension; and when they found themselves being briefed by a staff captain from Naval Intelligence in Cairo they realized their mission was going to be something out of the ordinary.

The staff captain wasted neither time nor words: "We've an important job for you two crews. Sit down, and I'll give you the general set-up first, then the details." As he unrolled a wall map of the coast of Cyrenaica the room became suddenly quiet.

"We've known for some time," the staff captain began, "that an Axis convoy is making for Tobruk—four Italian destroyers and four merchantmen—and we *thought* one of these merchantmen was the *Selina,* a ship we're especially anxious to see at the bottom. As you know, the squadron took off a couple of hours ago to deal with the convoy, and with any luck most of the ships by now will be sunk. But Intelligence have just come up with some bad news. They think the *Selina*— and that's the ship we *really* want—may have left the convoy after dark and be sailing by herself for Benghazi," he stabbed his stick at the wall map, "a couple of hundred miles to the west. Now the squadron will have made their attack by now, and it's too late to divert them on to the *Selina.* The R.A.F. doubt if their Wellingtons could find a single ship at night at a range of five hundred miles; and though they're laying on an attack at dawn we're afraid that by then the

Selina will have got to Benghazi. Only two standby planes are serviceable. We think you're the likeliest crews to see the job through. So it's up to you. We want this merchantman sunk."

There was a quickening of interest as their flight plan was unfolded in detail. Takeoff at one a.m.: a two-hour flight to the Bab-es-Serir (an oasis deep in the heart of the desert where they would refuel), then another two hours to the approaches to Benghazi. "And for Christ's sake," the briefing officer warned them, "keep clear of the area round the Blue Lagoon, about five miles northeast of Benghazi; apart from being the mouth of the River Styx—the old Greek's river of death—it's the site of Rommel's headquarters; there is a bloody great radio mast, and the place'll be stiff with flak." He went on to give them a detailed weather report (a depression was moving in from the central Mediterranean, and cloud and high winds were expected by dawn); he ran through their method of attack, their radio drill and their plans for a getaway; and finally he stressed the vital importance of their target being sent to the bottom. Crippling her, he said, was no good. She had to be sunk. And sunk well out to sea where there was no possible chance of salvage. He asked if there were any questions.

Cridland wanted to know what the *Selina* was carrying.

A couple of senior officers exchanged glances, and the staff captain shook his head: "I'm sorry," he said. "I can't tell you that."

Ken Richards asked if it would be safe to go in close. And the captain nodded: "The closer the better. She's not carrying ammunition or oil."

Half an hour later the air crew were walking out to their planes. Even in the short while they had been at briefing the weather had worsened, and the first faint whisper of wind was sighing in from the desert, stirring up the sand and cutting visibility to less than a mile. They didn't talk much as they walked across to the hard-standing where their Swordfish were warming up, though Peter did raise the question of the *Selina*'s cargo.

"I suppose," Cridland said, "it could be anything from tanks to V.I.P.s."

Ken shook his head: "If it was tanks or V.I.P.s I reckon they'd have told us."

"So what's your guess?"

"I'll let you know," he said, "when we get back." He regretted the words the moment they were out of his mouth. It was tempting fate.

They took off in a cloud of dust, came into formation over the airfield, and set course for the Bab-es-Serir.

Conditions for flying were not unpleasant; for though visibility on the ground had been reduced by wind-blown sand, at fifteen hundred feet the horizon was clear and the moon bright. Peter flew by his compass, knowing that if he deviated even a degree off course they would miss the one oasis in a thousand square miles of sand. But he wasn't unduly worried, for this was the sort of pinpoint navigation that he was used to—flying over the desert being very much like flying over the sea—and at the end of a couple of hours the palms of the Bab-es-Serir appeared exactly where he expected them over the rim of his cowling. They landed and taxied across to the trees in whose shade the drums of aviation fuel were stacked like gargantuan coconuts. Refuelling was slow, with every drop of petrol having to be filtered to keep out sand, and it was rising three-thirty before they were again on their way. On the second leg conditions were not so easy. For as they neared the coast and the Afrika Korps they were obliged to drop to ground level to avoid detection. And at ground level it was bumpy; the moon, hazed by dust, bathed the desert in a macabre light, and Peter and Cridland needed all their skill to avoid flying into the dunes and outcrops of rock which came streaming at them, blurred and distorted, out of the driving sand. Once they flew directly over a German laager; but in the embryo *ghibli* now building up throughout the desert they were out of sight before the machine guns could open fire.

They crossed the coast a little after five a.m., giving the Blue Lagoon a wide and very circumspect berth, and headed into the sea lanes north of Benghazi. Here, in the false grey dawn, they lay in wait for the *Selina.*

Cloud over the Gulf of Sidra was down to a thousand feet, and the wind was strong and laced with flurries of rain. Half hidden by cumulus the two planes flew up and down the approaches to the harbour, while the sky grew paler, the wind stronger, and the fuel drained slowly out of their tanks. This, to Peter, was the most nerve-racking time of all: like the wait in a boxing-ring corner before the bell.

It was Cridland who saw her first: a faint grey shadow, dwarfed by the phosphorescent gleam of her wake. She was about ten miles from Benghazi, and, to judge by the length of her wash, moving fast. They climbed into cloud and maneuvered up-wind, into a position from which the merchantman would be silhouetted against the waning disc of the moon . . .

Up to this point, Peter told his daughter, he could remember everything clearly. But the events of the next few hours were like a nightmare: a muddled sequence of events made terrifying by moments of all too vivid clarity . . .

They broke cloud simultaneously, either side of the *Selina*'s bow. Cridland was spotted first, and ack-ack spat at him angrily, and not the usual merchantman's pair of Bofors, but a whole broadside that tore open the startled sky.

"Jesus wept!" Ken's voice was sharp with fear. "She's more flak than a bloody battleship! Get in quick!"

He tried to. But his Swordfish wasn't built for speed. And in the twenty to thirty seconds before he could close, Cridland took the whole weight of the *Selina*'s fire. He could have avoided it by running for cloud; but it had been part of their plan that he should keep the merchantman occupied while Peter closed in undetected from the opposite bow; so he stayed in his dive, jinking, seesawing and side-slipping as the flak streamed up at him in solid curtains of white. Inevitably he was hit. He was hit again and again. But he didn't turn away. Wheels shot off, wing tips shredded, struts knocked loose and oil astream from his engine, he came on till a burst of incendiaries hit him flush in the fuel tank.

As Peter and Ken flattened out of their dive, they saw Cridland's Swordfish burst into flame, hang for a second against the paling sky, then plunge like a meteor into the Gulf of Sidra.

Peter was seized with a sudden anger. Up to now he had looked on the *Selina* as simply another target: an important target, it is true, but one to be bracketed in his mind with the laagers, gun emplacements and E-boats that he had been bombing on and off for the past six months. But Cridland's death made the merchantman something special. For Cridland had been his friend. Determination welled up in him, a determination that was cold as ice and concentrated as the beam of a spotlight. He rammed his nose down and his throttle up through the gate, and the Swordfish came plunging like an apocalyptic angel out of the night.

The merchantman saw him too late. Before her gunners could line up on a new target, he had closed to point-blank range; and as he squeezed his release button he knew his torpedo couldn't miss. He flung the plane through a hundred and eighty degrees and went snaking away, low, with ack-ack ricocheting round his tail. He waited. The seconds ticked agonizingly by. Then came the dull pulsating roar as his torpedo struck home. His anger left him as suddenly as it had come, left him drained of emotion and dangerously relaxed. Anxious to assess the damage, he pulled away from the protecting sea.

It was a mistake.

For although the merchantman was hit, her ack-ack had lost none of its venom, and before he could reach the safety of cloud a burst of flak exploded directly in front of him. There was a roar like a collapsing house; a reek of cordite; oil and smoke poured through their shattered windscreen, and their engine coughed, picked up for a moment and then cut dead. And there was no resurrecting it.

They spiralled down, the only sound the sad little moan of slipstream over their wings and the grate of a shattered propeller against the cowling. Fear pricked up the hair on Peter's neck. They were going to crash land in heavy seas and outside an enemy port; the best they could hope for was to be taken prisoner.

"Hang on, Ken! We're going to ditch."

Through the intercom he could hear his observer transmitting to Ma'aten Bagush: "SELINA TORPEDOED AMIDSHIPS. STOPPED AND ON FIRE. SINKING." But he hadn't time to worry about the *Selina*. He unplugged his helmet and looked for a place to touch down. There was not much alternative. In the thirty to forty seconds they would be able to stay airborne they hadn't a hope of reaching land; so he decided to ditch close to the *Selina* in the hope that they and the merchantman's crew would be rescued together. He turned into wind.

All too quickly the waves came rushing towards them, flecked with white and terrifyingly large. In a sea like this, he thought, we'll be lucky not to cartwheel on to our back. A tongue of flame, blinding in brilliance, licked suddenly out of the shattered cowling. He flung up an arm to guard his face. And the Swordfish quivered, stalled, and from thirty feet fell flush on the crest of a wave. The last thing he saw was the blood-red moon jerked like a puppet across the sky; then the world disintegrated round him in a maelstrom of noise and pain. He tried to tear off his harness and straps, but a shaft of agony knifed through his chest and his hands refused to move. He felt himself sinking. Water closed over his mouth. And choking and retching, he realized with an incredulous feeling of this-can't-be-happening-to-me that he was starting to drown.

The next thing he knew he was in the bottom of the Swordfish's dinghy, being violently sick.

It was Ken Richards who saved his life.

In the observer's cockpit the impact of ditching had been less, and Ken was no more than badly shaken. Within seconds of hitting the water he had fought clear of the plane and freed their inflatable dinghy from the wing. He was about to heave himself into it when he realized that Peter was still in the Swordfish. And the Swordfish was sinking. His every instinct screamed at him to paddle clear. But he didn't. He grabbed the fuselage, took a deep breath, and dived into the pilot's cockpit. As his fingers clawed at the safety harness, he felt the plane tremble and begin to spiral down—slowly at first and then with gathering momentum—to the bed of the sea. He forced himself to think clearly. He ran his fingers down the straps of Peter's harness, found the release gear, turned it and pressed it and felt, to his unutterable relief, the straps fall loose. He groped for his pilot, grasped him under the armpits and kicked for the surface. For a terrible moment their legs snarled up with the harness and control column and they were dragged down with the sinking plane; but with a desperate effort he kicked free, and they drifted slowly up, locked in each other's arms, out of darkness and into light.

They broke water almost beside the dinghy. Ken grabbed it, panting and retching, and clung to it tight as a dying man to the hand that is his only link with life; and after a couple of minutes his heart stopped pounding and the waves slipped back into focus and he realized he wasn't going to die—at least for the moment.

Peter never knew how much it cost his observer to haul him into the dinghy, how many times they capsized, how many times he drifted sinking away, how many times Ken very nearly gave up as he fought for his pilot's life among the uncaring waves. The first thing he remembered was being sick all over the bottom of the dinghy while pain knifed through his shoulder and chest. As if from another world he heard his observer's voice: "Steady, Pete! You're all right now."

"Urrrgh! Where are we?"

"In the dinghy. And doing fine. The wind's blowing us ashore."

"Did we get the *Selina*?"

Ken had been too preoccupied up to now to spare the merchantman more than a glance; but with Peter back to consciousness he took a more careful look at her: "Yes," he said slowly. "The *Selina*'s had it."

She was broken backed, low in the water, and flames were licking out of her hold. But her crew hadn't abandoned her. Half of them were battling with the fire while the other half fought frantically to load and lower her lifeboats.

From the dinghy Peter and Ken could see the whole scene with nightmare clarity, for the merchantman was less than a quarter of a mile away and spotlit by the glare of her flames.

A number of crates were being hauled on deck and loaded into her lifeboats: big, black and apparently heavy crates with some sort of design stamped in brass on their lids. It occurred to Ken that these crates might well contain the cargo which Intelligence had been so keen to see at the bottom—obviously there was something important in them, for the crew of the *Selina* were risking their lives to get them away. But it was a losing battle they were fighting. For even as Peter and Ken watched, the flames spread: great tongues of orange and gold which cast a flickering glow on the water and sent showers of sparks and columns of thin brown smoke high into the paling sky. The *Selina*'s captain, Ken thought, must be a brave man still to be thinking about his cargo.

The outsize for'd lifeboat (into which the crates had been loaded) crashed suddenly down from her davits. Men swarmed into her; her engine revved up, and she drew away from the blazing ship. A moment later the smaller after lifeboat was also swung out. But before it, too, could be lowered, a great pyramid of flame leapt out of the *Selina*'s funnel. For a second the whole ship and the men on her deck glowed white-hot and incandescent in the heat of the explosion. There was a reverberating roar. A column of slowly dispersing smoke. And the *Selina* vanished as if she had never been, her super-structure pulverized to dust as the flames touched off her magazines.

Peter covered his face; he rocked to and fro numb with shock, while Ken's fingers clamped tight on the gunwale and his lips moved in prayer.

The events of the next few hours had, to Peter, all the terror and confusion of delirium. He had broken his collar-bone; his face, and especially his eyes, had been burnt by flame and oil; and he had swallowed enough salt water to inflame the membrane of his lungs. He would have felt sorry for himself in hospital. In a corkscrewing dinghy that was lashed by spray and threatening any moment to capsize, he simply wanted to die.

But Ken Richards wouldn't let him. He gave him en-couragement and hope. "See the lifeboat, Pete—over there—we're better off than she is."

In the pale half-light they watched the *Selina*'s one sur-viving boat rising and falling among the waves. She was broached-to, overladen and unable to restart her engine which had obviously been flooded in the wash which followed the explosion. In her stern a tall bearded figure was giving orders, while her crew baled frantically and rearranged the crates. Ken shook his head: "They'd better dump those crates, or they'll founder."

They were driven inshore together, lifeboat and dinghy,

no more than a couple of hundred yards apart, while the grey of the sky gave way to mother of pearl and the clouds in the east flushed pink. After a while Ken gave a grunt of satisfaction: "Look, Pete! I can see the shore! We'll be there in a couple of hours."

Away in the southeast a faint grey line gained slowly in definition: the Libyan plateau. Ken unrolled their survival kit and pulled out a map and a pocket sextant: "That plateau's pretty high. And the wind's blowing us straight towards it."

"Where are we?"

"Somewhere north of Benghazi, about five or six miles offshore. I'll know more exactly when it's light enough for a fix."

The sky paled, the clouds broke up and lifted, and a flock of migrating birds flew high and silent into the dawn.

The two boats were less than a hundred yards apart, when the sun burst suddenly over the rim of the plateau—a great gold orb, framed at the moment of its appearance between two conical outcrops of rock. In an instant the coastline became alive, its trees, dunes and escarpments thrown into vivid relief. They could see a lighthouse almost dead ahead and a little farther along the coast a radio mast that was silhouetted like a needle against the disc of the sun. Balancing against the thwarts Ken turned the sextant on to its side and measured the angle between lighthouse and mast. He was settling down to work out their position when the squall hit them.

Neither of them had noticed that the water ahead had turned suddenly dark—for Ken was too preoccupied and Peter too dazed; and the first they knew of danger was the high-pitched shriek of the wind and the dinghy heeling over. They grabbed the lifelines and saw they were being swept into an area of broken water where the waves, whipped up by the line squall, swelled and burst in a turmoil of spray. Ken had barely time to throw out the drogue anchor; then they were clinging for their lives to the rubber gunwale as the wind howled and the dinghy twisted and swooped this way and that like an animal in convulsion. Several times they came within a hairbreadth of capsizing before the squall passed, and battered but safe they were spewed out into the calmer water which stretched away to the shore.

The lifeboat was not so lucky.

They could see she was doomed the moment the squall smacked into her. Already overladen and low in the water, she broached-to and started to founder. They could hear the frightened shouts of her crew. They could see them struggling to heave the crates over the side in a desperate effort to lighten her. But they were too late. One moment she was visible quite clearly, heeled over on the crest of a wave; the next she was gone, and the only sound was the hiss of the sea and the steady roar of the wind.

Peter lay huddled in the water at the bottom of the dinghy, cold and sick and shivering—he had seen too much in the last few hours of violence and death, and what happened after the foundering of the lifeboat he could remember only as one remembers a nightmare: a muddled series of events lit by moments of terrifying clarity.

He remembered Ken searching, without much hope, for survivors. He remembered his exclamation of surprise. "Hang on, Pete. We've visitors." He remembered the hands aclaw at the safety lines and the muttered *"grazie"* and *"danke."* Then the drogue was pulled in and the dinghy, once again, was being driven towards the shore, only more slowly now, with two waterlogged figures trailed in its wake. He remembered heaving himself up and peering into the faces of the men they had rescued. And the face of one them was to haunt him for the rest of his life.

There were two survivors: one Italian, one German. The Italian was pale and bearded, with grey eyes set unusually far apart and the epaulettes of a captain in the Italian Navy;

though injured and close to exhaustion, he still retained a certain dignity and the air of a man accustomed to command. But it was the other face that Peter was never to forget: the face of the German. It was a cruel, wedge-shaped face: pale eyes, slit lips and the square taut chin of a fanatic. They stared at each other over the rim of the gunwale; and though he was safe in the dinghy and the German hanging by his fingernails to a lifeline, Peter had the uncomfortable feeling that it was the man in the water who had the situation under control.

The sun climbed higher. Deadweight, the dinghy drifted towards the shore. Overloaded and waterlogged, they made slower and slower progress in spite of Ken's efforts to paddle and the survivors' to push.

Most of the time Peter lay huddled against the thwarts, only half conscious. His lungs ached and his eyes were beginning to seal up. After a while, as if from far away, he heard voices raised in anger. He couldn't imagine, at first, what was going on; then he realized that the two survivors had started an argument. He didn't speak Italian, so the words were meaningless; but it was clear that passions were running high.

"Tu non avresti mai dovuto caricare il canotto di salvataggio con l'oro." This, Peter could tell, was the voice of the German: sharp and incisive.

The Italian's voice was weaker, but equally sharp: *"Smettila di parlare del oro, imbecille. Gli inglese hanno visto dove è stato gettato in acqua."*

A moment of silence then: *"Quelli si possono far fuori. Si devono prendere prigionieri."*

"Ma ci hanno salvato la vita. Non si possono far fuori. Si devono prendere prigionieri."

The voices grew angrier. It seemed a crazy time, to Peter, to start an argument, when they had literally only a fingerhold on life. He glanced at Ken. His observer was baling: baling and listening with the preoccupied look of a man who has found the solution to a problem, and, having found it, is suddenly afraid.

Fingers aclaw at the gunwale. A thud. A choking cry: "*Vigliacco!*" Then silence.

Ken peered angrily over the side: "Hey! What's going on?"

The German's English was halting: "The *capitano* he has —how do you name it—the gramp. He let go. He is carried away."

"Hmmm!"

It didn't sound a very likely story to Peter; but his observer seemed to accept it, and if the men from the *Selina* wanted to fight and drown each other it was no concern of his; he couldn't care less. He shut his eyes, sliding once more into a semicoma of exhaustion and pain.

In silence they drifted slowly towards the shore, now hazed in sunlight and mercifully close.

It was a little after midday that they grounded quietly on a sandbar at the mouth of what Peter later discovered was the Blue Lagoon.

After more than four hours in the water the German was almost at the end of his tether. Ken had to help him ashore, and it was while he was half dragging him up the gently shelving beach that he noticed his uniform: it was the uniform of a lieutenant in the Gestapo.

They left him and staggered a little way along the coast to where a cluster of date palms leaned over the lagoon. Everything was very peaceful: just the sun, the sand, the wind in the palms, and away at the entrance to the lagoon a black robed Arab, oblivious to the ebb and flow of war, fishing from his *gaiassa.* In the far distance Ken could make out the thin grey line of a road, with the occasional truck grinding along it under a haze of dust. But Peter couldn't see the road, for his eyes had sealed up.

He tried to persuade his observer to leave him, to make an effort to get back to Ma'aten Bagush. But Ken wouldn't hear of it: "Me. Walk four hundred miles with no one to drive me! You're joking . . . Now listen, Pete. We're bound to be captured. And questioned. And you've *got* to remember something."

"What?"

"Say nothing about seeing the lifeboat sink. And nothing about my taking the bearings. Say you can't remember *anything* after we ditched."

He nodded, too dazed to wonder why.

It was while they were resting exhausted under the palms that Peter first had the dream: the dream that was later to haunt him night after night in the hospital in Tripoli. The trouble started when he gathered from a chance remark of his observer's that it was the Blue Lagoon into which they had drifted: the spot where the River Styx of Greek mythology entered the sea. And it was soon after this, when Peter was on the threshold of delirium, that the fisherman in the *gaiassa* became metamorphosed in his mind to Charon (the boatman who, according to the ancient Greeks, ferried the dead over the River Styx). The fact that he was half blind made the metamorphosis all the more vivid, the fisherman's black robes seeming to take on the texture of a shroud, and his face assuming the featureless white of a death mask. He screwed up his eyes and tried to scrabble away from the water. "Don't let him near me!" Ken Richards, who could make neither head nor tail of his pilot's babbling, was almost glad when he saw the German lieutenant dragging himself over the sandhills that led to the road; for he knew then that capture was only a matter of time.

After a while Peter's weakness temporarily left him, and his delirium brought on a feverish energy. He grabbed his observer's arm: "Let's get out of this."

"Be sensible. We can't walk four hundred miles to Bagush."

"We can try."

Ken Richards sighed. He knew they hadn't a chance. But

it was useless to argue with a man in the throes of delirium. He took Peter by the hand and they set off together along the shore of the lagoon. They were thirsty, the sun was hot and Peter kept tripping over little protuberances in the sand. But he refused to give up.

They had covered rather less than a five-hundredth of the distance to Ma'aten Bagush when, inevitably, they were spotted.

They arrived on the back of a Tiger Mark II: six privates and a sergeant in the grey peaked caps of the Afrika Korps. They bundled Peter and Ken on to the tank and drove to Rommel's headquarters. They were none too gentle at first; but when they saw that Peter was blind and injured they did what they could to make him comfortable.

Peter could remember little about their interrogation, except for its terrifying climax. Lost in a world of darkness and pain, he had a vague recollection of being asked, not ungently, a great number of questions and replying over and over again: "My name is Peter Grey. I'm a sub-lieutenant in the Fleet Air Arm. And that is all I can tell you." Then a new voice took over the questioning. It was a voice that he recognized, sharp and incisive: the voice of the man they had rescued, the lieutenant in the Gestapo. When he refused to answer he was ordered to stand to attention, and the bright white light of an arc was flashed into his injured eyes. He heard a voice screaming again and again, "You bastard, I'll tell you nothing"; he remembered feeling surprised and indignant that his voice was so high-pitched; he heard his observer cursing, their first interrogator protesting, and the sharp reply of the lieutenant. Then the door was flung open, and a sentry bellowed the sort of "attention" that in any army heralds the arrival of a senior officer. He could see nothing, but he understood sufficient German to get the gist of the conversation that followed.

"So these are the men who sank the *Selina?*" the newcomer's voice had a soft Bavarian burr.

"Yes, *Herr General.*"

A pause, then: "That man is injured."

"He is blinded, but we think only temporarily."

"Have both men dismissed and their injuries seen to."

"Herr General!" Up to now the talking had been done by their first interrogator, but this was the voice of the lieutenant.

"Yes?"

"I think these men could help us. They may have bearings on where the boat went down. I suggest they are handed over to my department, for special questioning."

There was a long silence. Peter could feel the sweat breaking out on his forehead. Then—almost too wonderful to be believed—came their reprieve. "The war in North Africa, Lieutenant Schultz, is a clean war. We have no use in the desert for the special skills of the Gestapo." A pause, then: "That man will go to Italy as a prisoner of war, that man to hospital. At once. And I hold you responsible that no harm shall come to them. Do I make myself clear?"

A dissatisfied grunt from the lieutenant, and Ken Richard's voice as if from far away, *"Danke, General Rommel"*; then the tiredness and pain that Peter had dammed back for so long swept over him; there was a great roaring in his ears; his legs crumbled; and he spun round and down, down and round into a merciful oblivion.

The next thing he saw, when three weeks later they took the bandages off his eyes, was the domed and ornately frescoed ceiling of the military hospital in Tripoli.

"And that," he said to his daughter with a self-deprecating smile, "is how Daddy won the war!"

For a while she was silent, staring into the dying fire; then she said slowly: "You didn't keep in touch with Ken, after the war?"

"I did to start with. His parents had been killed in the blitz. He'd no relatives in England. And when he got back from Germany he came and lived for a while with my parents. We were pretty close in those days. But when your mother and I married, Ken drifted off. He borrowed a couple of hundred pounds—a hell of a lot of money in those days—and went dashing off to Italy. Then he moved on to South America—Tierra del Fuego, I think. And you know how it is. For years we swapped Christmas cards, then we drifted apart."

"What a waste."

There was nothing he could say to that. But her next remark took him by surprise: "You won't go to Lob's Wood, will you?"

"Good heavens, Anne! Why ever not?"

"Please, Daddy. Don't get mixed up in anything."

"I promise you," he said, "I know far too much about the law to get mixed up in anything shady."

Her fingers twisted at her handkerchief: "But it's bound to be shady, or dangerous. You don't get offered a million pounds for nothing. Just like that."

A log fell off the fire, flared briefly, then crumbled to ash. It was past midnight and the room was cold. "I wonder," he said slowly, "what the *Selina* was carrying."

"I've an idea we'd be happier if you never found out."

"But of course I want to find out."

They were on different wavelengths: she attuned to the need of preserving their home, he with his ear on the beat of a distant and more exciting drum; and they both had more than a streak of obstinacy. At one a.m., with nothing settled, he banked up the fire, put the dog in its kennel, and went to bed. But his daughter stayed in the sitting room playing Beethoven's Twenty-third Sonata.

From his bedroom he could hear the music quite clearly,

the troubled notes of the Appassionata streaming like storm-tossed leaves through the night. And he couldn't sleep. As a bar of moonlight moved silver across the wall of his room, he thought back to the days when he and Ken had shared the skies of another and more stimulating world, and it seemed a far cry from the rigors and delights of the desert to his unexciting offices in Lincoln's Inn.

He realized after a while that the tempo of the music had changed. She was playing the Eighth Sonata now, the Pathétique, and playing it with an eloquence that would have brought tears to the eyes of a man more prone to show his emotions. She's got talent, he thought; all that she needs is time and money, time to study and money to pay her fees at a *conservatoire*. The trouble was that with motherless children to care for, time and money had in the last five years been in short supply, and his daughter had been forced to spend too much of her time on the chores of running a home. He reached for his observer's letter. *And if the idea of becoming a millionaire appeals to you* . . . Was it, he wondered, too much to hope that here was the opportunity he had been longing for for years? The opportunity for Anne to escape the host of her household chores and the opportunity for him to break away from his humdrum life as a commuter—a life which seemed to have become progressively dissatisfying since the death of his wife. He was calculating what time he would need to leave the office to reach Lob's Wood by six-thirty, when he fell asleep.

THE GOLDEN OYSTER

CHAPTER 1

LOB'S WOOD HOTEL is set a little way back from the Farnham to Tilford road; it used to be James Barrie's house, and the trees of old Lob's Wood (where everyone had his second chance) still form a background to one of the loveliest gardens in Surrey. He arrived a few minutes after six-thirty, parked his battered old Mini beside a Maserati Mistrale, and walked into the bar.

It wasn't especially full. Two locals drinking bitter at the far end of the counter, an elderly couple enjoying a quiet sherry, and at a table by the French windows a very attractive girl who wouldn't, Peter guessed, be sitting by herself for long. He asked for a light ale, and the barman smiled: "Would you be Mr. Peter Grey?"

"That's me."

"Your friend's outside on the terrace. Through the French windows."

He was carrying out his drink, when his eyes met the girl's. She was, he decided, even more attractive than he had first thought: a model's figure, dark hair, blue wide-apart eyes that reminded him of someone else's (though he couldn't for the moment think whose), and the sort of suntan that one doesn't come by in England; and she was smiling at him. He smiled politely back in a way that seemed to amuse her, then he was through the French windows and looking round for his observer.

Ken Richards was lost in contemplation of the pines of Lob's Wood: the tall, loose-limbed figure that he remembered so well, his face more lined and his hair turning grey, but unmistakably his wartime observer. When he saw Peter his eyes lit up: "My favourite pilot! It's good to see you!"

As they shook hands, Peter eyed him appraisingly. He looked fit and prosperous: a suntan that owed nothing to bottles, and a new and discreetly well-cut suit.

"Shall we stay outside, Pete? Where it's quiet?"

They sat themselves on the wall of the terrace, looking out over carefully tended lawns to the woods beyond. It was a lovely evening: a scent of resin and the garden warm and somnolent in the soft gold light of the sun. Peter sipped his beer. "I'm not sure that I understood your letter."

"Let's not rush our fences. How's the world been treating you? How's Jean and the family?"

"The family are fine. Jean was killed five years ago, in a car crash."

"Oh, Pete! I *am* sorry. I wish words weren't so damned inadequate." A pause, then: "How do you cope with the kids?"

"Anne's a great help, and we have a housekeeper on and off. We're very lucky really."

"Damned expensive I should think, a housekeeper."

He ran a hand through his hair. "You're telling me! What with her wages, three lots of school fees, and Anne wanting to study music, it's a job to keep our heads above water."

"But you've got your work as a solicitor. I bet that's interesting."

"It's a living."

"Nothing more?"

"Let's say it's a rut I'm getting tired of running along. But what about *you?* You're looking on top of the world."

Ken Richards, it seemed, had been everywhere, done everything: whaling in the Antarctic, oil surveying in Central America, investing in real estate in British Columbia and working for Voluntary Services Overseas. It was to the last of these that he had, in recent years, given his heart; and as he talked to Peter of his work in Tierra del Fuego his voice took on the concern of a shepherd whose flock is threatened by unseasonable snow: "You've no idea of conditions down on the Straits of Magellan. It's unbelievable. About the worst climate on earth. And a whole race slipping back into the Stone Age, dying slowly of exposure and malnutrition."

"Hmmm! You've certainly got around. But you haven't got around yet to explaining that letter!"

The sun dipped under the pines and the garden grew suddenly darker. Ken Richards looked for a place where they wouldn't be overheard. The terrace was within earshot of the bar; in the car park a couple in the Mistrale were oblivious to the world; but the garden was deserted.

As they strolled up and down the lawn, midway between hotel and woods, Ken lit his pipe: "Have you ever heard," he asked between puffs, "of the Rommel treasure?"

"No . . . Oh, wait a moment: I believe I *did* hear rumours . . . Wasn't there suposed to be a shipload of gold lost in the war? Somewhere off North Africa?"

"That's right. Off Benghazi."

"Benghazi! I seem to remember it was Tripoli."

"The papers *did* mention Tripoli at the time. But this was a cover-up story, put out by the people doing the salvage."

"I see."

A skein of geese on their way to Frensham Ponds went honking low over the pine woods. And the penny dropped.

"So the gold went down off *Benghazi!* You don't mean it was in the *Selina?*"

"It was."

He felt like a man brought suddenly face to face with a complex jigsaw; he could see that the pieces might very well fit together, but he couldn't see how. "Tell me slowly," he said, "step by step."

Ken Richards drew on his pipe. "If you think back, there was obviously *something* pretty valuable in the *Selina.* Remember how cagey Intelligence were about her cargo. And remember how her crew risked their lives to salvage the crates. I wondered at the time what was in them. And the chaps we picked up from the lifeboat let the cat out of the bag . . ."

"Of course, you could understand Italian!"

"Enough to get the hang of what they were quarrelling about: one of them said, 'You should never have loaded the gold into the lifeboat'; and the other, the big chap with the beard, said, 'Stop talking about the gold, you fool. The English saw where it was dumped' . . . Well, this was a pretty substantial clue, and after the war, armed with your two hundred pounds, I went to Italy and unearthed the whole story. It's all in Italian N.I.D. papers. The tonnage of the *Selina*—5,365 tons; the name of her skipper—Carlo Tacchini, a captain in the Navy; and the composition of her cargo—around three million pounds in gold, two million pounds in paper currency, and over one million in jewels and *objets d'art.* The whole lot was being shipped to Libya partly to pay the Afrika Korps and partly with the idea that as soon as Rommel got to Cairo—and everyone, you remember, thought he was *bound* to get there in those days—he'd use it to buy Intelligence and support in the Middle East." He relit his pipe. "Now six million pounds is a fair bait, and by the time I got to Italy there'd already been two attempts at salvage. Divers had located the hull of the *Selina* in about fifty fathoms. They had no end of a job getting down to her—working at that sort of depth is absolute hell—and you can guess what they found."

"Nothing?"

"Not a single *louis d'or*. For the very good reason that the Rommel treasure isn't in the wreck of the *Selina* at all. It's in the wreck of her lifeboat. And that went down a good deal nearer the shore."

"But surely someone's discovered the lifeboat by now?"

"How can they? When I'm the only person in the world who knows where it is."

"Say that again!"

"Think back, Pete, to that morning in the dinghy. Cridland and Strong went down in flames—they hadn't a hope of surviving. The *Selina* exploded—remember how she went up in a cloud of dust; no one could have survived *that*. Her only survivors were the men in the lifeboat. Now remember what happened? As the sun came over the plateau I took a couple of bearings to fix our position. And a moment later we were hit by the squall, and the lifeboat, which was close behind us, capsized, and her crew were drowned. In other words those bearings I took fix not only *our* position, but also the position of the treasure."

"Now I *am* beginning to see."

"We picked up two survivors from the lifeboat: the Italian captain and that bastard from the Gestapo. The Italian never got ashore—I've a pretty good idea why. Which means there are only three people alive who can possibly know that the treasure went down in the lifeboat, and only one person, me, who can pinpoint the lifeboat's position."

A twilight breeze sighed soft through the pines, and the shadows of Lob's Wood advanced like thunderheads over the lawn.

"But if you know where the gold is why on earth haven't you gone and got it?"

He laughed: "It's not as easy as that! Oh, I could have

sold the bearings any time to the Italian government, watched the salvaging and collected ten per cent of the profits. But I'm a gambler. I want the lot—what couldn't I do with two or three million pounds down on the Straits of Magellan! Twice during the fifties I took a team with the latest diving equipment out to the Gulf of Sidra. But you've no idea of the technical difficulties. The lifeboat is in over three hundred feet of water and almost certainly covered with sand. The currents are tricky. And in spite of having the bearings, we couldn't locate the crates let alone raise them. And I came to the conclusion that with existing methods of diving, a small team had very little chance of salvage. So I waited. And waited. And about six months ago the waiting paid off."

"Go on."

"Diving techniques, you see, had been improving all the time, and eventually I got in touch with a chap called Gary Malloy, who's done a lot of experimental work with deep-sea capsules. And to cut a long story short Malloy and I have gone into partnership. We reckon with his equipment and my knowledge we'll have the treasure up by the end of the year."

It was part of Peter Grey's job to find flaws in the stories that people told him, but he couldn't find the flaw in this one. "I think," he said slowly, "you're in danger of becoming a millionaire! But why, after all these years, contact me?"

"You were in at the beginning: and now I'm sure the treasure *can* be raised, I thought you'd like to be in at the end. Six million pounds splits nicely into three."

"But Ken! I can't offer you any sort of *quid pro quo*."

"I wouldn't say that. But don't make a thing of it. Come along for the sake of auld lang syne. I ought to warn you though: there *could* be danger."

His daughter's warning came home to roost. "Danger? Who from?"

"From our friend Lieutenant Schultz."

For a moment the name meant nothing; then came memories of the pale eyes and the clipped, incisive voice, and he shivered: "Is *he* after the treasure too?"

"Lieutenant Schultz," his observer said dryly, "is an elusive character. He's wanted by the War Crimes Commission. And by the police, who think he's mixed up with the Mafia. And I've a pretty shrewd idea that he's got his eye on the treasure."

"Have you actually seen him?"

"Once, when Malloy and I were in Benghazi. And since then my room's been ransacked a couple of times. And I've been followed."

"You weren't followed here? Tonight?"

"I doubt it, unless he put Jim Clark on my tail!"

"What's he after?"

"The bearings."

"Good God, man, you don't carry them on you?"

Ken Richards laughed. "I'm not *quite* such a fool. They're in the safest place I could think of: my solicitor's vaults."

"All the same, you'd better watch your step. Who *are* your solicitors?"

Ken pulled a diary out of his pocket and thumbed through the pages: "I always forget half their names! Here we are: Edwards, Knight, McInnes and Burkinshaw, 16 Eastcheap, London, E.C.3."

Peter made a note in his address book. He was returning the book in his pocket when Ken's fingers clamped tight on his arm. "Quiet!"

In the woods away to their right a twig snapped sharp as the cock of a gun, and a pheasant rose startled out of the heather. For a moment they froze. Then a girl laughed, and down through the pine woods, hand in hand, came the couple from the Mistrale. When they saw Peter and Ken they hesitated, then veered off in a detour back to their car.

Peter eyed them thoughtfully. "They were too far off," he said, "to have heard."

Ken nodded, but his hands as he picked up his tankard were none too steady. "I've talked myself dry!"

They made for the bar. By common consent they had talked enough of the Rommel treasure; and for the rest of the evening they relived in a roseate haze the exciting days of the war. The bar was crowded, and it was quite a while before Peter noticed with surprise that the dark-haired girl was still sitting beside the windows, alone, and drinking, of all the unlikely drinks, a cup of coffee. He stared at her, vaguely—for a reason he couldn't account for—puzzled and disturbed; and when their eyes met across the haze of tobacco and beer, it was he who looked away.

They didn't mention the treasure again until a couple of hours later when they were standing beside their cars. Then Peter said quietly, "There's something I want to know."

"Which is?"

"Why you're cutting me in. You and Malloy could handle this yourselves."

Ken Richards scraped a pattern in the gravel with the toe of his shoe. "After Colditz I was on my beam ends, physically and mentally. I'd lost everything: parents, home, the lot. You were more than good to me, Pete. You put me back on my feet. You even lent me a couple of hundred pounds when you and Jean were scraping together literally every halfpenny to buy a house—and it was that two hundred, by the way, that enabled me to go to Italy and start the search. So it's like I said in my letter: the bread that you cast on the water is being returned. And there's another reason for bringing you in. We had a reputation in the old days, as a crew: a reputation for seeing things through. People don't change. You may have lost a bit of hair and put on three or four inches around the waist. But when it comes to the crunch I know you're not the sort to throw up the sponge. And that sort of quality *could* be mighty useful."

Silence, and a bat flitting darkly among the pines. Then, "What about this chap Malloy?"

"What about him?"

"*He* won't like my coming in."

"I made it very clear to Gary Malloy when we drew up our contract that I might have a partner, and that proceeds would have to be split three ways. This he accepts."

A longer silence, then: "I'm tempted, Ken. God knows I *want* to come. But I've responsibilities: three motherless kids on my hands . . . Can I sleep on it?"

"Sure. I'll tell you what. Sleep on it tonight. And tomorrow would you look into a bit of legal problem for us?"

"What's the problem?"

For several minutes they talked of the laws of treasure trove and salvage; then, when Peter was quite sure that he understood what his observer wanted, he promised to have an answer within twenty-four hours.

"Grand. I'll phone tomorrow evening. And if you're still in doubt I suggest we meet Malloy. He's quite a character."

And that was the way they left it, with Ken promising to telephone the following night when he had confirmed where and when the three of them were to meet.

It was midnight before he was home and reading the note that his daughter had left on the hall table: "Tigger is in his kennel. Wendy's tooth came out and is under her pillow; can you swap it for a sixpence? When I went in she was still awake."

He climbed the stairs and tiptoed to the side of his younger daughter's bed. She lay on her back in the moonlight, her hair fanned out on the pillow and her arm crooked awkwardly round the neck of her bear. For a while he stood looking down at her, thinking of all the teddy bears that the Rommel treasure could buy her, and all the school fees it could guarantee for Richard, and all the music tuition for Anne. Then he felt in his pocket for sixpence. He thought at first that he hadn't got one; but when he shook out his address book the little silver coin fell to the floor. Putting down the address book on the table by Wendy's bed, he recovered the sixpence, slipped it under the pillow and extracted his daughter's microscopic tooth.

Half an hour later he was asleep: asleep and dreaming: dreaming of seas of Mediterranean blue and crates of *louis d'or*. Once, sharp and incongruous, the barking of a dog brought him to the threshold of consciousness. But the barking ended as suddenly as it had begun, and he drifted back to the shore of his dreams where gold-filled crates rose tempting out of the sand.

CHAPTER 2

It was the scream that woke him, the terrified scream of a child.

He jerked up in bed, trembling, sweat on his palms. Sunlight was pouring in through the window, the hands of the mantelpiece clock were at six fifty-five, and the screaming went on and on.

He tumbled out of bed and on to the landing and saw Wendy, clutching her teddy bear, stumbling up the stairs. Her eyes were screwed tight and her screams had the ring of hysteria. He picked her up. For a moment she fought him blindly, her hard little fists pounding his face; then, realizing who he was, she clung to him tightly, sobbing as if her heart would break.

"It's all right, Wendy." He carried her back to his bed and lay beside her under the cool rough sheets, smoothing her hair. But it was a long time before he was able to get through to her. "What's the matter, darling?"

"Tigger! Oh poor Tigger!"

"What's the matter with Tigger?"

Her tears ran warm down his neck. "He's been run over."

As soon as she was sufficiently in control of herself to be left with Anne he hurried to the dog's kennel. When he saw what had happened sickness welled up in his throat and he thought he was going to faint. Tigger hadn't been run over. He had been killed: and killed with a wanton brutality that pricked up the hair on Peter's neck. For his throat had been cut and his body mutilated. As if in a dream he fetched a tarpaulin from the garage and laid it over what had once been a dog. He was walking back to the house, cold with anger and shock, when Richard came tumbling out of the front door. "Dad! We've had burglars!"

He went quickly from room to room, the children trailing openmouthed in his wake. The house had been searched, and searched by someone who had made not the slightest effort to cover his tracks. The papers from Peter's desk had been tossed into a heap, drawers were left open, and the contents of cupboards left strewn over the floor. Yet nothing, it seemed, had been stolen.

"Richard and Wendy"—his voice was grim—"don't touch anything. I'm getting the police."

He glanced at his watch; it was only a little after seven o'clock, and the village constable was likely still to be at home. He went upstairs for his address book, where he had a note of the constable's private number.

The address book, however, was not in its usual place (together with his fountain pen, wallet and loose change on the chest of drawers in his bedroom) nor was it in the pocket of the suit he had worn the night before. For a moment he couldn't think what he had done with it. Then he remembered: he had put it down on the table by Wendy's bed. It never occurred to him as he went into her room that the book wouldn't still be where he had left it. But it wasn't. There was, however, something else by Wendy's bed: a bloodstain, a smear of russet standing out like an angry bruise on the cream paint.

He stood very still, fear building up in him like water behind a dam; for he was able quite suddenly to visualize what had happened in the night as clearly as if he had tailed the intruder from room to room . . . Ken *had* been followed to Lob's Wood. His shadower had watched the two of them as they walked the hotel lawns, and had seen them pull out address book and diary. In point of fact all that Peter had made a note of was the address of his friend's solicitor's, but he could just as easily have been making a note of the bearings. And the shadower, intrigued, had transferred his attention from Ken to Peter. He had followed him home. In the small hours of the night he had broken into the house. Tigger, after a single bark, had been silenced. And the intruder had gone from room to room, searching. Eventually he had come upstairs. And in Wendy's room he had found what he had been looking for: the address book.

Was it, Peter wondered, Shultz himself? He could picture the scene with nightmare clarity: the man with the pale cruel eyes, with Tigger's blood still wet on his knife, standing beside his daughter's bed. And it came to him in a moment of intuition that the mutilation of his dog had been no act of casual brutality, but a deliberate warning: a warning to those who led sheltered lives not to stray into the jungle.

With a lot of men it would have worked. But Peter wasn't the sort to be intimidated and kicked around. Bastards, he thought, as he asked for a line to the local police station. They'll not get away with this.

The police were not inclined to treat his story all that seriously at first, but when he showed them the body of the dog their attitude changed. Not much was said; but the set of the sergeant's mouth as he pulled aside the tarpaulin was more eloquent than words. He spent nearly an hour helping the police as much as he could—telling them enough of the truth to explain the burglary and mutilation, but not disclosing the whereabouts of the treasure—and before he left for London he had their assurance that they would keep a round-the-clock watch on his house.

Anne was unusually quiet as she drove him to the station. It was clear she had a pretty shrewd idea that Tigger's death and the loss of the address book were tied up with his visit to Lob's Wood; it was clear too that she heartily disapproved of whatever it was he was getting involved in. But she didn't indulge in recriminations. And for this he was grateful: "I'll explain everything this evening, Anne. When the little ones are in bed."

She nodded. She came with him on to the platform and kissed him good-bye as though she might never kiss him again. "Take care," her voice was slightly breathless, "that you don't get pushed under a bus!"

"I promise I won't go near one."

Her anxiety heightened his awareness of danger. But nothing his daughter did or said would have made him alter his mind. His mind was made up. It was the savaging of his dog that had tipped the scales. And once in the offices of Blake, Son and Sturman he cancelled his appointments and set to work on the problem that Ken had outlined.

There were, in fact, two problems rather than one. Firstly, assuming that they managed to raise the treasure, would it be legally theirs? And secondly, assuming the treasure *was* theirs, how could they legally and safely convert it into usable currency? It was essential, Ken had told him, that these points were cleared up before they left for Benghazi.

The first problem was the simpler, and he soon tracked down a ruling: "In the absence of proven ownership treasure recovered from the open sea becomes the property of the finder, who gains a title to it which is good against all claimants." So the only problem here was whether the *Selina*'s lifeboat had gone down in "open sea." She had, according to Ken, foundered five or six miles offshore; and after checking that the limit of Libyan territorial waters was only three miles, Peter concluded that outside this the sea would be classified as international and hence by definition open.

The second problem was not so simple. For he soon realized that even if they managed to raise the treasure and load it on to a salvage ship, their troubles would be far from over. What country would they take it to? And how would they avoid the possibility of being hijacked by Schultz and his colleagues en route? The obvious place to which to take it was England or America; but America involved a long sea voyage and a heavy tax, while in England as soon as the gold was brought inside the three-mile limit it would become crown property. There were ports in the Mediterranean such as Tangier and Beirut which were conveniently close to Benghazi and where the gold could be sold without formality; but there would be far more risk in such a port of their being hijacked. For a long time it seemed to Peter that the expedition's small size and unofficial status precluded safety, while import and tax regulations throughout the world precluded their enjoying more than a very small percentage of whatever treasure they raised. But round about the time that his secretary brought in tea, he had the germ of an idea. A series of phone calls to the continent and the idea crystallized, and by five p.m. he had the draft of a report which he knew would meet his observer's needs. He put it on tape, locked the tape in the safe, and managed to scramble on to his usual train.

His whole family were waiting at the car park; for in spite of the watch on their house Anne had decided not to leave the little ones by themselves. He thought they all looked tired and strained, and it came to him in a moment of contrition that while he had been pleasantly occupied in the office, his children passed the day in the shadow of things not easily forgotten. He made a special effort when they got to Dragonfly Cottage to take their minds off the events of the previous night. He bathed Wendy himself, and let the smaller ones watch the telly and stay up for supper. It was nine o'clock before he and Anne were able to sit down to the talk for which he knew she was longing.

He stoked up the fire. "Any phone calls?"

She shook her head.

"Ken Richards'll be ringing soon . . . Now, I'll put you in the picture."

He told her everything.

Her reaction was much as he expected. "It's a wonderful story, Daddy. And a wonderful opportunity for Ken. But don't *you* get involved."

"There's a million pounds at stake."

"Money isn't everything."

"No"—he sighed—"but it's damned hard to do without it. And a hundredth of what we've been offered would get you to Siena."

Her eyes clouded. "You promised never to mention Siena. I've told you: I don't care whether I go or not."

He knew that it wasn't true. He knew that she was ambitious and talented, that she longed to take up the chance she had been offered to study at one of the best *conservatoires* in Europe, and that she only *said* she didn't want to because, up to now, there had not been the slightest chance of their affording the fees. "But surely"—he adopted the ever-so reasonable tone that he reserved for his more obstinate clients—"surely this is the chance of a lifetime."

Her lips tightened. "Suppose Wendy gets the Tigger treatment? She'd look nice, wouldn't she, with a leg by the window, an arm by the door, and her head stuck on the bedpost!"

"Stop that, Anne."

"Oh, Daddy! Be a realist! People who play with fire get burned."

"You children," he said slowly, "wouldn't be in the slightest danger. It's me they're trying to warn off, not you. You could stay with Aunt Audrey. Or, better still, with that friend of Nannie's in Cornwall. What was her name? Mrs. Lovesay. No one could possibly trace you there."

Her fingers twisted tight round her handkerchief. "I don't think," she said slowly, "I could cope with the little ones, by myself."

He stared at her, reminded suddenly of Jean; when *she* had set her mind on something she had fought the same way, with every weapon but tears. He reached for her hand. "Please, Anne. Don't make excuses. Just say *why* you don't want me to go."

A lump of coal flared suddenly green as the flames licked through to a vein of pyrites. She wouldn't look at him; her voice was so low that he had to lean forward to hear what she was saying. "Surely you know."

"But I don't."

"Oh, Daddy! Do I have to spell it out! Think of all the things that could happen to you."

He felt a surge of affection. It hadn't occured to him that her fear was on *his* account. "You needn't worry about me," he said lightly. "I'm old enough to look after myself."

"But these men are dangerous. Think what they did to Tigger." She smiled at him sadly, "You're not James Bond, you know."

"I'm well aware," he said, "of my limitations. I promise to sleep with only one girl a night."

She wasn't amused: "But we're so safe and happy as we are. We've a home, plenty to eat and each other. Why risk losing the lot?"

"One's got to accept *some* risk," he said slowly, "to get hold of a million pounds. And think what the money would mean to us. *Your* chance to follow a vocation. *Richard's* chance to get to a public school. *My* chance to opt once and for all out of the rat race."

They argued the moon halfway across the sky. But they found no easy solution. It was eleven-thirty when Peter looked suddenly at his watch. "What on earth's happened to Ken?"

She stared at him blankly.

"Ken Richards. He promised to ring this evening."

The thread of their argument broken, they sat for a while in silence, while outside the cottage mist hung damp in the hollows of the hills and a policeman's torch cut a swathe of white through the darkness as a deer fled bounding over the moon-bright fields.

"I promise you," he said at last, "that I won't do anything silly. I won't take part in anything illegal, or in a wild-goose chase. I'll reserve judgment till I've met this Gary Malloy. And if there's anything I don't like about the setup I'll back out."

And with this she had the good sense to be content.

They went to bed at midnight, with Peter by this time more than a little anxious over his observer's failure to telephone. For quite a while he lay awake, watching the moon cast kaleidoscopic shadows on the wall of his room and thinking how strange it was that such a very ordinary person as himself should have got involved in such very unordinary events; but round about one o'clock tiredness got the better of anxiety and he fell into a restless sleep.

It was the telephone that woke him. He switched on the bedside light and peered, bleary-eyed, at his watch. The time was a little after three a.m.

Anne answered the phone while he was still struggling into a dressing gown. As he opened the door on to the landing, her voice came clearly up the stairs: "Dorking 5811 . . . No, this is his daughter . . . Saint Thomas's Hospital! Yes, he's just here." Her eyes, as she passed him the receiver, were frightened.

"Peter Grey speaking."

It was a businesslike, faintly foreign voice that came over the line. "This is the casualty department of Saint Thomas's

Hospital. I'm sorry to bother you, sir, at this time of night: but I understand you are a friend of Mr. Kenneth Richards?"

"That's right."

"Mr. Richards has been brought into casualty with head injuries. He has been asking, most urgently, to see you. And I wondered if you could possibly come to the hospital?"

He felt as he had felt that morning twenty-five years ago when Cridland's Swordfish had spun blazing into the Gulf of Sidra: cold, angry and filled with a single-minded determination. First his dog and now his friend. He'd make them pay, somehow, if he had to follow them to the ends of the earth. "Is he seriously hurt?"

The voice became guarded. "Head injuries, sir, are always treated as serious. But he's not on the danger list, at the moment."

It was the "at the moment" that decided him. "I'll come right away."

As he replaced the receiver his eyes met his daughter's. He half expected recriminations and tears or at least an "I told told you so"; but she simply said, "You dress. I'll get coffee."

It was while he was halfway through shaving that the idea suddenly occurred to him. He unplugged the Ronson and walked thoughtfully to the top of the stairs: "Anne!"

"Yes?"

"Could you phone Saint Thomas's, please? To be sure it *was* them."

"I've already checked. The call was O.K."

Though strangers to the jungle they were learning fast. And before Peter left for London he took yet another precaution: he had a word with the policeman watching the house. Then he was driving fast into the dawn.

The roads were deserted, and in less than an hour he was parking the Mini outside Saint Thomas's.

He had unhappy memories of hospitals—though the doctors hadn't given her a chance in a thousand, Jean had clung to life for almost a week, and the echoing corridors and the smell of antiseptics brought back a heartache that the years did nothing to dim. After a brief wait in casualty-clearance he was taken to the Pakistani doctor who had been on duty when Ken was brought in.

At about ten o'clock, the doctor told him, the hospital had received a phone call to say there had been a burglary in Thackeray Street, Kensington, and a man had been beaten up with an iron bar. When the ambulance men arrived they found the flat ransacked, and Ken unconscious on the floor with his head in the lap of a young Italian girl who was trying to staunch the blood from a gash in his temple. They had brought him to the casualty ward—the girl coming too, and not leaving until they had assured her that Ken's life was not in danger. The doctors had been afraid at first that his skull was cracked, but X rays seemed to indicate that it was no more than badly bruised. His left eardrum, however, had been split, and there was a danger that his hearing might be permanently damaged; he also had several minor injuries, including a badly bruised arm and a fractured bone in his wrist.

The moment he regained consciousness he had asked for Peter.

The doctor smiled. "And when we do not produce you like the rabbit out of the hat, your friend becomes excited, almost hysterical. We gave him sedatives, but they had little effect. Now as perhaps you know, Mr. Grey, in brain injuries it is important for the patient not to be under mental stress. So we telephoned you, and I am very happy you were able to come."

"Ken Richards and I are old friends."

"So I understand. And now you can see him. There is something worrying him, and if you could put his mind at rest this would be most beneficial. In fact"—the doctor looked at him carefully—"I would go so far as to say that if his mind is *not* put at rest the consequences might be very serious indeed."

"I'll do what I can."

Ken Richards had been put in a private room—the girl who came with him in the ambulance had apparently asked for this. He was lying on his back with his head swathed in bandages; but he was fully conscious, and when he saw his pilot his eyes lit up. He grabbed Peter's arm and tried to lever himself out of bed; his voice was high-pitched and his eyes kept rolling out of focus. "Pete! Get my wallet. See if there's a paper in it: with a diagram and figures."

There was plenty of money in the wallet; but no paper with a diagram and figures.

Ken cursed. "God damn it! They've got the bearings."

"Take it easy, Ken. Lie down and tell me what happened. Slowly."

It came out in an unco-ordinated rush. "Last night in my room, I was working out a search from the salvage ship, with the bearings all laid off, when someone knocked on the door. I asked who it was, and a voice called out, 'It's Sally from the flat downstairs.' I thought it was O.K. because I recognized her voice. So I stuffed the papers into my wallet and unlocked the door. She was standing there with eyes like saucers and a man with a knife to her throat. I tried to slam the door shut, but they jumped me, three of them. I caught the first chap a crack on the jaw. Then one of the others hit me over the head with a sort of bar. He kept on hitting me again and again, and I thought, my God he's going to kill me. Then somebody shouted 'Police!' and I passed out."

"What do you remember next?"

"Lying on the floor of the sitting room—it looked like a cyclone had hit it—and a girl trying to stop the blood running into my eyes."

"What girl? Sally?"

"No." He frowned: "I don't *think* I'd seen her before.

Attractive little piece—dark hair, blue eyes and, a crucifix. She wasn't in uniform, but I thought she might be a nurse."

"What made you think that?"

"She seemed to know what she was doing. And she said something about Saint Thomas's."

"That's where you are now. So take it easy and relax."

"How *can* I relax!" His voice rose and little globules of sweat ran down his forehead and into his eyes. "I added ten degrees to the bearings. But a clever man could cotton on to that. Schultz could be off to Benghazi, now, while I lie here like a useless hulk."

"There's no need to get so excited. You said yourself: no one's likely to raise the treasure without Malloy's special equipment."

His eyes were too bright and his fingers clamped too tight on the frame of his bed. "That's what I hope. But I want to be sure. Promise me something, Pete!"

"What?"

"Oh don't be so damned cautious! Promise."

It was against his every instinct; but the voice of the Pakistani doctor came drifting in with the hum of the air conditioning: "in fact if his mind is *not* put at rest the consequences might be very serious indeed." "All right," he said, "I promise."

"Don't wait for me. Get the bearings from McInnes and Burkinshaw. And go after the treasure yourselves. You and Malloy."

He didn't hesitate. How could he, even if he had wanted to, with the sweat standing out in beads on his observer's face and his eyes rolling out of focus? He reached for his hand. "Of course we'll go. I'll see Malloy right away, this afternoon."

Ken Richards lay back. It was as if a great weight had been lifted suddenly from his injured brain. He closed his eyes.

The tempo of his breathing relaxed. And when a nurse looked in a few minutes later he was asleep.

But Peter, as he walked the dew-wet pavements in search of an early breakfast, was thoughtful. For he was committed now: committed beyond recall to walking a road which he knew would take him far from the staid and respectable confines of Lincoln's Inn.

CHAPTER 3

HE arrived at the Dorchester at three forty-five. He knew that Malloy was American, rich and an expert on the latest techniques of deep-sea diving, and he had built up a picture of him in his mind—a cross between Papa Hemingway and Jacques-Yves Cousteau; but the man who welcomed him into his suite didn't fit the picture. Malloy was frailer and older than he had expected: a mild-mannered man of rising sixty who looked, in spite of his mahogany tan, as though he would be more at home at a desk than on the bed of the sea.

"So you've decided to come treasure hunting, Mr. Grey?" The American's smile was friendly and his handshake firm, but the eyes that summed his visitor up were watchful.

Peter had made up his mind that he wasn't going to rush things. "When I saw Ken Richards," he said slowly, "I was pretty well forced to tell him we'd leave for Benghazi as soon as we could."

"And you're now regretting that?"

"Let's say I'm anxious to know in a little more detail what's involved."

Malloy nodded. "You'll join me for tea?"

It was brought to the suite: silver tea pot, china cups, and paper-thin bread and butter that would have delighted the ladies of a more leisured age. For a while they talked trivialities; then Malloy steered the conversation to a subject in which he knew that Peter would feel at home. "Ken told you, I think, that we've a bit of a legal problem?"

"He did. And I believe I've got the answer . . . In the case of treasure reclaimed from open sea the law's simple." He pulled a sheaf of typewritten papers out of his briefcase. "Here are the authorities and precedents. It's all straightforward, and once the treasure's raised it'll unquestionably be ours—at least while we keep it on the high seas. The only possible snag would be if the Libyan government extend their territorial waters."

"Are they likely to?"

"They'll probably try sooner or later, especially now they're prospecting for oil in the Gulf of Sidra. But they've not petitioned the United Nations yet, and these things take months to push through."

"O.K. So we raise the treasure and it's ours. But how do we convert it to hundred-dollar bills?"

"That's not so easy. In my opinion if we tried to sell the gold in a port like Beirut or Tangier, we'd very likely end up with a knife in our back. If we took it almost anywhere else, we'd forfeit the bulk of it in duty and tax. I say 'almost' because there *is* one country in the world that's enlightened enough not to confiscate wealth but encourage it . . ."

"Switzerland?"

"Exactly. So it's my suggestion we fly the gold to Zurich or Geneva, and declare it and put it into a numbered account in the Banque Helvétia. All we'd have to pay would be a seven per cent import duty. No tax. No questions."

Malloy looked at him with interest: "That makes sense. But how do we get the gold from Benghazi to Switzerland?"

"I suggest we sail it to Malta, unload it into a bonded

warehouse and then fly it on, with a special guard, at our leisure—say by B.E.A."

"No duty at Malta?"

"Not for goods in transit. They can be put into bond for up to fourteen days."

A long silence, then. "Your very sound suggestions, Mr. Grey, could save us literally millions of pounds. I hope that after giving us all this good advice you're going to join us?"

Peter stubbed out his cigarette. "Before I give you my decision," he said slowly, "there're a couple of points I'd like to be absolutely clear on."

"Which are?"

"First, what makes you so sure you can raise the treasure? I mean what's so special about your equipment that you think you'll succeed where everyone else has failed?"

Malloy unlocked a drawer in his desk and handed Peter a folder. "Would you care to glance at these? Details of *Oyster* and *Pearl*: my research ship and her deep-sea capsule."

"What I'd prefer, Mr. Malloy—if you've got the patience—is a step-by-step explanation of exactly how you plan to conduct the salvage operations: as from now."

"Sure." Malloy leaned back in his chair. "I reckon it would take us at least a week to tie things up in England. I've equipment to collect from your Navy yard in Portsmouth, and you —assuming you're coming—you'll have your family to settle and visas and passports to see to. Then I'd suggest *you* fly to Switzerland and sort things out with the Banque Helvétia, while *I* move on to Monte Carlo—that's where *Oyster* is berthed.

"She's a fine ship, especially designed for underwater exploration: length a hundred and ten feet, beam twenty-three feet, draft eight foot six inches and a cruising speed of over eleven knots." Malloy reeled off the figures with the relish of a connoisseur who boasts of his mistress's statistics. "She's got a crew of twelve, including divers: all men who have sailed with me before and are a hundred per cent trustworthy. We'd need three or four days to get to Benghazi; you could join us there; and we'd be ready to start operations. Our first job would be to locate the lifeboat. Ken's bearings—which by the way we'll have to collect from his solicitors—would be the key here. The lifeboat must have gone down within say half a mile of the position he plotted. So we'd mark off an area to be searched and comb it thoroughly section by section, towing a magnetometer."

"That's a sort of detector?"

"Sure. It picks up kinks in the earth's magnetic field that are caused by extraneous metal. It's a sophisticated gadget to operate; it's got a limited range and it can't be used in any sort of sea, so the search could take weeks or even months. But we'd be ninety-nine per cent certain to locate the lifeboat in the end. And once we'd located her, the rest would be easy. We'd anchor directly above her and lower *Pearl*—that's the deep-sea capsule. Now have you any idea how she operates?"

He shook his head.

"Have you heard of Ed Link and his deep-sea capsule? Or Cousteau and his house under the sea?"

"I've heard of *them*—they've been in the news quite often the last few years."

"Well, *Pearl* works on the same principle as Link's capsule. Let's say the treasure is three hundred feet under water. What with pressure, narcosis, the bends, carbon dioxide poisoning and the limited amount of breathing mixture it's possible to carry, that's far too deep for normal divers to operate in in either comfort or safety for more than a few seconds. But with *Pearl* it's simple. Two men climb into her. They are sealed up and fed through air pipes with the right mixture of oxygen and helium for the depth they want to work at—in this case three hundred feet. *Pearl* is then lowered from the research ship. When she gets to three hundred feet she stops. The men climb out through an air lock, and being already acclimatized and pressurized to the depth to which they've been lowered, they can at once move about quite freely on the bed of the sea—provided of course they go on breathing the same mixture of oxygen and helium through the air pipes and stay at the same depth. You see the beauty of it! No cumbersome diving suits. No limit—apart from cold and fatigue—to the time they stay down. And when they want to come up they simply climb into *Pearl,* seal themselves in and are hauled to the surface. Decompression, of course, once they're back in the research ship, takes time—twenty-four hours or even forty-eight hours. But the divers needn't stay in the capsule for this; they can crawl through the air lock and into a big decompression chamber where they're brought back to normal in comfort while the capsule, with other men in her, can be lowered again and again."

Peter was impressed. He was by no means technically minded; but it was obvious that Malloy knew his subject and what he said made sense. "So with the help of this capsule the actual raising of the treasure ought to be easy?"

"The divers can simply go down in her, load the gold into nets and we'll winch it up. I'd say we could raise the lot in twenty-four hours, provided there aren't any snags, like bad weather."

"Or interference from Schultz?"

A pause: then, "I have set my heart, Mr. Grey, on raising the treasure. It will take more than a Nazi war criminal to turn me aside."

Peter looked at him curiously; it was his first indication that Malloy might not be as meek and mild as he looked. "You're a rich man," he said slowly, "why does the treasure mean so much to you?"

Malloy studied his fingertips. "I have no wife," he said at last, "and no child. When I retired four years ago I wanted something to do. It had to be something worthwhile—collecting butterflies or kidding myself I was Picasso didn't appeal to me. It was the fascinating work of Cousteau and Link that opened my eyes to the wonderful world that's under the sea. Has it ever occurred to you, Mr. Grey, how little we know of what lies under the sea? The seabed comprises seven-tenths of the surface of the world, and yet we've no more than scratched at the fringe of it. We shoot cameras thirty million miles into space to film the wonders of Venus, but the wonders that lie a couple of hundred yards offshore have escaped us. It's taken me four years and the best part of half a million dollars to perfect *Oyster* and her equipment. Up to now I've done only little jobs in her—filming underwater coral in the Marianas and searching for sunken wrecks in the Caribbean. But this is something big. Think of the publicity if we raise the Rommel treasure! Think of the boost to my equipment and methods of deep-sea exploration! And—make no mistake—this is a worthwhile cause. For I'm convinced that man's research would be best directed not at space but the sea; and any little thing I can do to give impetus to deep-sea exploration will be a service to humanity. But all this," he laughed self-consciously, "can weigh very little with you. What was the other point you wanted to talk over?"

Peter walked to the window. It was the rush hour and buses and cars were jammed tight the length of Park Lane. He stubbed out his cigarette. He needed the extra few seconds to get things sorted out in his mind; and by the time the smoke had stopped rising he knew what he wanted to say.

"I wonder what our chances are?" His voice was thoughtful. "Everyone who sets out on a treasure hunt must reckon he's on to a good thing; but ninety-nine per cent end up disappointed. I wonder how much danger there is—from the sea: from our friend Lieutenant Schultz? Probably more than we realize. The point I'm trying to make is that we may end up empty-handed or dead. Now you and Ken have only yourselves to think of. But I've three children who've lost their mother. Imagine how they'd be placed if I was killed."

For a while Malloy was silent. Then he said slowly. "Say I offered you a salary, three thousand dollars a month for a minimum of three months; and a covenant of thirty thousand dollars for each of your kids in the event of your being killed or disabled?"

He was considerably taken aback. "Terms like that," he said with alacrity, "would be far too generous to refuse."

Malloy held out his hand. "I'm determined, Mr. Grey, to raise this Rommel treasure. I reckon you'd be a useful man to have around, especially now that your navigator's out of action. And there's another point"—the smile extended now to his eyes—"I've an idea that you and I won't get too much in each other's hair; and that, believe me, on the sort of expedition we're planning, is a matter of some importance."

They talked for a couple of hours of plans, safeguards and technicalities. Then, after Peter had telephoned his daughter to say he would be home late, they cemented their partnership in the muted light of the Dorchester's cocktail bar.

He got back to Dragonfly Cottage a little after nine, to find Anne unusually subdued. The watch on their house, she told him, had been doubled since the attack on Ken Richards. "There's one policeman in the kitchen swigging tea, and another snooping about in the woods like Sherlock Holmes!"

He couldn't think of anything to say that would not add fuel to the flames of her discontent.

There was Lancashire hot-pot in the oven, a cheerful fire in the inglenook and a pile of his favourite sonatas stacked up on the piano. He was afraid for a moment that she might have deliberately set the scene for a heart-searching talk on why-leave-such-a-happy-home? But she was way ahead of him.

"When," she asked quietly halfway through the meal, "are you going?"

"In about a week."

"If I asked you *why* you were going, would you tell me?"

"I'd try."

"You've always been honest with me, Daddy. Please be honest now."

He was relieved that she apparently accepted his decision. "Honestly, Anne," he heard himself saying, "there isn't just one big reason, there's a whole lot of little ones . . . I'm going, first, because I want the money; think of all the things we could do with it—and that includes packing you off to Siena! Second"—he went on quickly, afraid that she was about to interrupt—"second, I'm going because I made a promise to Ken, and I don't want to sound pi about this but when a man's saved your life it makes the promise you give him even more binding than usual. Third, I'm going because I like Malloy and I respect his judgment, and if he says we've every chance of success I believe him. Fourth, I'm going because if we don't raise the treasure Shultz and the Mafia will; Shultz is a murderer and a war criminal, and the Mafia deal in brothels, drug peddling, protection and murder; and think of the harm six million pounds would do in *their* hands. And last, to be quite honest, I'm going because I *want* to go." He split up the coal in the hearth with unnecessary vigour. "Maybe at forty-plus, I ought to be happy to spend the rest of my life commuting to a drab little office and gardening and sitting at home by the fire; but there *are* more exciting ways of living. Besides, I'm damned if I'll sit on my bottom and do nothing while a bunch of thugs mutilate my dog and bash in my best friend's head . . . After which long speech for the defence I hope your Honour is satisfied?"

"If not satisfied at least sympathetic . . . Look"— her fingers drummed at the keys of the piano—"you're going. Full stop. But please, oh please be careful you don't get hurt. You're not playing the lead, you know, in a script where the hero always ducks at the right moment. The men who carved up Tigger and battered Ken on the head would cheerfully put out your eyes for a tenth of the Rommel treasure. Now I won't cry when you go. I'll look after Richard and Wendy and we'll be fine. But don't imagine we'll say thank you for all the gold in the damned *Selina* if anything happens to *you* . . . After which long summing up, the case is closed and your Honour intends to play the piano until the early hours of the morning."

She chose the pieces that she knew he liked best: the Moonlight Sonata, the Chopin Nocturnes, and, as he got ready for bed, Rachmaninov's Rhapsody on a Theme of Paganini. He would have liked to sit listening by firelight (as he often did) into the small hours, but he was dog-tired and his eyes kept dropping shut, and a little after eleven o'clock he said goodnight and climbed the stairs and tumbled exhausted into pajamas and bed.

But the notes of the Rhapsody still haunted him, drifting through his bedroom window with the muted light of the moon. She was playing it beautifully, with a clarity and control that made him realize she was keeping her emotions on a tight rein. Poor kid, he thought, she's not had much of a life these last five years. But things'll be different soon. And thinking of all that Siena would mean to her, he fell asleep.

He didn't wake when at two a.m. she tiptoed into his room.

She stood looking down at him. She thought he looked old and vulnerable, with his face lined and his hair flecked grey: not at all the sort of man to exchange knife thrusts with the Mafia three hundred feet under the sea. She bent down and kissed him very gently on the mouth.

He reached out, forgetful of the years that had passed, for Jean. When he found there was no one beside him, he sighed and rolled over with his face to the wall.

CHAPTER 4

It took them ten days to tie up the loose ends: to sort out their vaccinations and visas, to open negotiations with the Banque Helvétia, to buy their final items of equipment and for Peter to hand in his resignation to Blake, Son and Sturman and get the children safely installed in Mrs. Lovesay's cottage in Cornwall—their move to the West Country being planned like a military maneuver, with Peter indulging in the most elaborate subterfuge to ensure that his family couldn't be traced. Mrs. Lovesay was an old friend of the Nannie who had helped to look after Richard, a contact remote enough to be almost impossible to trace and yet well enough known to the family to be a hundred per cent reliable. Peter could rest assured that with her the children would be both cared for and safe.

And every evening either he or Malloy paid a visit to Saint Thomas's.

Ken Richards, much to their relief, made a surprisingly rapid recovery. For the first couple of days his eyes had been wayward to focus and his hearing deranged. But the electroencephalogram confirmed that his brain had escaped injury, and on the third day the doctors told him he had been lucky and that provided he convalesced sensibly there should be no lasting ill effects. Indeed, on the day before Peter was due to fly to Geneva, he was already talking about his discharge. Peter was surprised. "A bit early, I'd have thought, to be letting you out?"

Ken looked smug. "They say next week as long as I behave myself. I expect they need the beds."

"Hmmm! Where'll you convalesce?"

"I've a married sister in Dublin—you remember Jenny. Or I might try Newton Driver's."

"And for how long?"

He pulled a wry face. "No swimming, flying or violent exercise for a couple of months. This"—he gestured to his arm—"in plaster for three weeks. And this"—he tapped his ear—"wrapped up in cotton wool for six. And no alcohol!"

"Quel ennui!"

"But it won't be for ever. You'd better look sharp at raising the gold, or I'll be out there chasing you up!"

"Don't," Peter said quickly, "start getting silly ideas."

But he was very much afraid, from the way his observer smiled, that the ideas had already taken root.

He left for Geneva the following morning.

It was cool and still, with the sun not yet powerful enough to have penetrated the haze, as he strapped himself into the Viscount. He couldn't quite believe at first that he was saying *au revoir*—and maybe good-bye—to his family, his home, the rush hour and the hemmed-in offices of Lincoln's Inn; but as the Viscount rose smoothly away from its shadow, he realized in a moment of consternation-cum-elation that the search for the Rommel treasure was under way.

He felt uneasy to start with: like a yachtsman venturing for the first time into unknown waters; but as the fields of Picardie gave way to the vineyards of Champagne, the anxieties of the last few days ebbed gradually away and he began to relax. This, he told himself as the air hostess brought him a pre-lunch Martini, was vastly preferable to the daily grind of Blake, Son and Sturman: this was Life. Soon he could see the Alps, a long unbroken chain of snow-capped peaks aglint in the sun; then the arc of Lake Geneva, gentian blue and speckled with sail. He peered at it eagerly. The last time he had walked the shores of Lake Geneva had been eleven years ago, with Jean.

An hour later he was settled into his comfortable room in the Hotel du Rhône.

He expected to spend a couple of days in Geneva. In fact he spent six. For the Swiss, unused to dealing with sunken gold, moved cautiously. They were not unhelpful, merely painstaking and excessively thorough. He had to admit, however, that at the end of it all, the arrangements they laid on for unloading and banking the gold couldn't be faulted.

The delay meant, among other things, that he missed his direct flight to Benghazi and had to travel to Rome to pick up a B.O.A.C. Comet; and it was three weeks to a day from the time he first saw Ken Richards' letter to the time he was looking down once again at the Libyan escarpment.

It was a quiet evening as the Comet lost height over the Gulf of Sidra: the sea was a picture postcard blue, cloud was hanging like a necklace above the shore, and the desert pulsated with colour—ochre, claret and gold. As they passed over the harbour Peter peered down at the shipping in the hope of catching a glimpse of *Oyster*. The harbour, he noticed, had been considerably enlarged since the war; in the commercial basin to the north some half-dozen merchantmen were unloading beside the quays, while the basin to the south was crowded with yachts, dinghies and fishing boats. Among the latter was a white flat-sterned vessel that *could* have been *Oyster*; but it disappeared under the Comet's wing before he had time to catch more than glimpse of it.

Much to his delight the first person he saw as he came

through the customs was Gary Malloy. His luggage was piled into the back of a waiting Mercedes, and within minutes of touchdown they were speeding along the long straight ribbon of road that led from airport to town.

It was a ten mile drive to Benghazi through more or less virgin desert. The desert hadn't changed: the red sand, the tired palms and the all-pervading dust, it brought back memories. As they bumped along in the light of a dying sun Peter pointed out the Rommel Pool—site of the Afrika Korps headquarters where he and Ken (was it really more than twenty-five years ago!) had been questioned—and that brought back memories too. But when they came to the city, there was hardly a thing he could recognize; for the battered and fly-blown pile of rubble, which had changed hands five times in the war, had been replaced by a booming metropolis: broad streets and demi-skyscrapers, cinemas, snack bars and night-clubs. For oil, after two thousand years, was bringing back prosperity to the one-time Garden of the Hesperides. Benghazi, Malloy told him, was now one of the most expensive cities in the world to live in. "Reminds me of Caracas," he grumbled. "You can't get a decent meal under ten bucks!" He parked outside the Yacht Club and pointed. "There she is."

She was moored about fifty yards offshore, well clear of other shipping: a sleek efficient-looking vessel of rising a hundred tons. They went out to her in one of her boats.

As Peter clambered aboard, the awning over the quarter-deck screened off the light of the sun, and it was a couple of seconds before his eyes became acclimatized to the gloom. He had a vague impression of deck chairs and tables, surrounded by tier after tier of diving equipment. Then a man was rising out of one of the chairs: a tall loose-limbed man with his head in bandages and his arm in a sling. He couldn't believe his eyes. "Ken! How the devil did *you* get here?"

"By oil tanker. A couple of hours before you."

Malloy was grinning from ear to ear, like the amateur conjuror who has managed to haul a rabbit out of his hat. "I suggest we have our explanations," he said, "over a nice cool cocktail—except for our unexpected guest who'll drink Mineralé and like it!"

As the sun dipped under the harbour wall and the lights of the town flickered gold in the sea, Ken Richards explained what had happened.

There was no great mystery, he told them. There had, needless to say, been a telephone in his room at Saint Thomas's, and from there he had made his plans with the connivance of a friend in the oil industry. He had managed to persuade the hospital to send him home the day after Peter had left for Geneva; the moment he was discharged, he had hired a car and been driven straight to Fawley; here he had boarded an oil tanker that was due to sail later that night for the Libyan oil terminal of Marsa Brega. The voyage, he said, had been a complete rest cure, and had done him good rather than harm. He had arrived in Libya this morning, had been driven straight to Benghazi and had presented himself aboard *Oyster* only a couple of hours before his pilot. He had no intention, he told them, of doing anything strenuous: like work. He had simply come to sit and watch them raising the treasure. It would be exactly what Saint Thomas's had recommended: a nice quiet Mediterranean cruise!

They went to their cabins early. And it wasn't until he was on the borderline of sleep that Peter realized how glad he was that his observer was with them. There was a rightness about it: that the two of them who together had seen the treasure go down should now years later be seeing it raised. He shut his eyes and listened to the slap of waves on their hull and the jingling bells of horse-drawn carts on the quay, and could hardly wait for dawn.

CHAPTER 5

HE woke to the mew of gulls and the throb of engines: not, he realized after a while, *Oyster*'s engines, but those of a vessel alongside. Pulling on sandals and shorts, he clambered on deck.

In the half-light of dawn Ken Richards was arguing with a voluble and persistent Italian in a red-striped jersey whose trawler was nuzzling their gunwale and who seemed to be trying to sell them fish. Eventually, more to get rid of him than anything, Ken bought a basket of mullet, and the trawler pulled away. She was a clumsy powerful vessel, manned by a crew of some half a dozen who, it seemed to Peter, were taking a more than passing interest in *Oyster*'s diving equipment. He wasn't sorry to see the last of them as they disappeared round the wall of the outer harbour.

They discussed their plan of campaign over breakfast.

Malloy had been in Benghazi for several days, and while waiting for Peter he hadn't been idle. His first concern had been to make sure that Schultz and the Mafia had not already tried their hand at salvage. And on this count the police and the port officials were reassuring: no new divers or salvage vessels, they said, had been working recently from Benghazi; the only diving along the Cyrenaican coast had been done by a fleet of Greek shallow-water sponge boats who came each autumn to work in the Gulf of Bomba. His second concern had been to reconnoiter the search area; and together with *Oyster*'s skipper—a bearded Scot of few words but many accomplishments—he had used Ken's bearings to calculate and mark off on their charts the area that would need to be combed. He had also tested their equipment.

"So," Ken's voice was eager, "let's go!"

An hour later they were heading for the sea lanes north of Benghazi.

It was a lovely morning: an inshore breeze, a clear sky and no more than a hint of swell; perfect conditions for towing the magnetometer. On their way to the search area Malloy showed Peter and Ken round the ship and introduced them to the crew.

They were amazed at the quantity and complexity of *Oyster*'s equipment. The bridge was packed with radars, D/F equipment, chronometers, gyrocompasses and depth recorders. The forty-foot working space aft was crowded with air hoses and compressors, magnetometers, compression chamber, *Pearl,* marker buoys, cylinders of oxygen and helium and tier after tier of skin suits, fins and aqualungs. While the engine room was impressive as a warship's: twin diesels, which gave a cruising speed of eleven knots and a top speed of well over twenty—"If we step on the juice," Malloy told them with pride, "there's hardly a ship in the Mediterranean able to catch us." Their tour of inspection ended beside an improvised gun room which was unlocked to reveal a rack of Winchester rifles and Biochiarelli shark guns, together with a supply of powerful underwater grenades—none of which, Peter profoundly hoped, would ever be used.

As for the crew, they appeared to be as well-found as the ship. There were ten of them. Torquil McArthur the skipper, monosyllabic but far from morose behind his beard; Scott-Henderson the doctor, whose bedside manner (they were later to learn) remained inviolate in crisis; two engineers, one for the diesels and one for the diving gear; a radar-cum-radio operator; four divers; and a cheerful five-foot Indonesian cook whom Malloy laughingly introduced as "Fanny Farmer." Peter totted them up. "I thought you'd a crew of twelve."

Malloy nodded. "We *should* have been twelve, but a couple of divers couldn't come at the last minute. And I didn't want to sign on anyone new."

"Will four divers be enough?"—this was Ken.

"Should be. The rest of us can take a turn if we have to. With *Pearl* to go down in, there's practically nothing to it!"

An order from the master and *Oyster* lost way. Another order, and she hove to on the edge of the search area.

Peter found it hard to believe that he had been here before, huddled half-delirious with pain on the floor of a corkscrewing dinghy. It looked so different now, so peaceful, the sea and the shore asmile in the warmth of the sun.

They studied the chart, where Ken's observations had been laid off in a spider's web of tangent and bearing. Malloy had worked things out with meticulous accuracy, identifying all the landmarks that Ken had taken a sight on. He *thought* he had plotted the dinghy's position (and hence the treasure's) to within a couple of hundred yards. But time would tell.

"Would you say we're in the right spot, Peter?" Malloy was watching him anxiously.

He frowned. "A bit close inshore, I'd have thought."

"Mr. McArthur. Would you lower a boat?"

A couple of minutes later Peter was eyeing the coastline again, this time from the floorboards of *Oyster*'s dinghy. He was amazed. From sea level his view was far more restricted than it had been from the deck of the salvage vessel, and the coastline appeared to have receded and taken on a familiar flatness. He could identify the lighthouse that Ken had used for a bearing, its flashing beam pinpricking the line of the Barce escarpment, also the conical outcrops of rock between which the sun, that morning twenty-five years ago, had risen. And the whole scene suddenly took on such a familiarity that he almost expected to hear the high-pitched shriek of the line squall and the hiss of the sea as it closed over the capsizing lifeboat. "This is the spot." His voice was confident.

They positioned the first of their buoys. They paid out the magnetometer. They switched on radar and depth finders, and moved slowly to the southeast corner of the area they planned to search.

It was not a big area, little more than half a mile square; but it would take them, Malloy had estimated, the better part of a fortnight to comb it. For they had to tow the magnetometer at only half a knot, and in parallel runs of less than five yards apart. It was a job that called for pinpoint navigation, precise control of the magnetometer and endless patience. They lowered another marker buoy and started the first of their long, slow, nerve-racking runs.

To start with, everyone was keyed up, glued to the magnetometer's recording screen like novitiates to television. But as the hours passed and run succeeded run and there was not so much as a flicker from the needle, their enthusiasm gave way to a more realistic resignation.

It was going to be a long job.

They organized watches: two men to cope with navigation and two to operate the magnetometer, while the rest settled down to sunbathe, tinker about with their equipment or swim.

A little after midday they were joined by one of the sponge divers they had seen in Benghazi: a forty-foot converted trawler which started to work the shallows a couple of miles inshore. Through binoculars they could see her crew diving among the sandbars and coming up, every now and then, with sponges the size of balloons. They would have been happier if she had chosen other shallows in which to work, but they could hardly ask her to move on.

Peter spent most of the day flaked out on his back in the bow, alternately reading and sunbathing. There wasn't much to look at: the occasional flying fish with its fast-beating wings aglint in the sun as it skimmed clear of their bow, the odd biscuit-coloured sponge floating by on the surface, and once, a few feet underwater, a glum-looking turtle swimming purposefully towards the shore. It was all very peaceful.

They continued their runs until sunset, with no sign of movement from the needle of the magnetometer. Then, in the short subtropic twilight, not wanting to be caught alone at night in the open sea, they headed back for Benghazi. They had combed, McArthur calculated, rather less than a twelfth of the search area.

By seven o'clock they had secured to a buoy well clear of other shipping, and by eight had squared off for the night. Though they told themselves they could hardly have expected to find the treasure on the very first day, they were conscious of a slight feeling of anticlimax.

They were about to turn in when the Italian trawler that had sold them the mullet came nosing into harbour. She threaded her way towards them and dropped anchor disconcertingly close. After a while they noticed that a man in her wheelhouse was studying them through binoculars.

Malloy, McArthur, Peter and Ken held a conference in the saloon. So long as they were in a floodlit harbour and surrounded by other shipping they reckoned there was little danger. But Benghazi wasn't Monte Carlo or Cowes; they were taking no chances; and they decided that night and every night to mount a double watch with two armed men patrolling *Oyster*'s deck. It was comforting, as they lay in their bunks, to hear the tread of the patrol: round and round, up and down, while the moon hung gold over the desert and the hum of the city faded to the occasional clatter of taxi and snatch of song.

And the night was uneventful.

Malloy, anxious to comb as much of the area as possible while the weather held fine, had them up next morning an hour before sunup. By seven o'clock they were starting the first of their runs.

Hour after hour they towed the magnetometer through waters calm as a dew pond, watched first by the occasional gull and later by their shadow, the sponge diver. It struck them as rather more than a coincidence that the sponge diver should be working the same area as *Oyster* for the second day in succession; but at least she kept a respectful distance and took no apparent interest in what they were doing. And the only excitement that second day was provided by their antics in the water.

One of the divers had started a cold, which precluded his descending to any depth, and Malloy suggested that everyone (apart from Ken) should make as many practice descents as possible in case they needed a standby.

Peter was no expert at deep sea diving; but he had spent many summer holidays pottering about with his children in flippers, mask and snorkel, and he was pleasantly surprised to find how quickly he adapted himself to the aqualung equipment and to breathing a mixture of oxygen and helium. He didn't go down in the capsule that first afternoon, but stayed at a comparatively shallow depth, chaperoned by Al Grindly, the senior diver—a former instructor in the U.S. Marines. To start with, he had his work cut out to regulate his depth, equalize the pressure in his ears and carry out one or two simple drills. But as he gained confidence, he began to enjoy himself. It was an exhilarating feeling, drifting weightless as a cosmonaut through a strange blue world: and he was quite disappointed when at the end of an hour his companion pointed upwards and it was time to follow their air bubbles to the surface.

Too soon it was twilight, with *Oyster* again heading for Benghazi. All day the needle of the magnetometer had been limp as a rag doll; but at least they had something to show for their efforts; for on McArthur's chart exactly a fifth of the search area had been screened off.

They had hoped on the third day to make another early start. But during the night the weather took a turn for the worse, and they woke to the grey skies and swirling sand of a *ghibli*. It was frustrating. They hung about all morning listening to the steady roar of the wind and watching the sky for signs of a clearance. But no clearance came. Malloy was philosophical. "Rather the *ghibli*," he said, "than the Mafia. And at least there's no sign of *them*."

But he spoke too soon.

It came when they were least expecting it: the warning that the ice on which they were skating was thin.

Late in the evening Peter and Ken went ashore to buy fresh fruit and vegetables. As they made their way down the the harbour wall, en route for the market in the Souk el Jerid, they passed the Italian trawler that had sold them the mullet. Looking down they could recognize her skipper in his red-striped jersey; he was mending nets with the help of a girl. As they passed, the girl, hearing footsteps on the quay above her, glanced up.

They both recognized her at the same moment: the blue wide-apart eyes that had held Peter's across the crowded bar at Lob's Wood; the crucifix that had swung from her breast as she staunched Ken's blood on the floor of his ransacked flat.

For a moment the three of them stared at each other, unmoving, a little tableau spotlit by the light of the trawler's arc. The girl smiled. And her smile was as charming as the rest of her: "Hello there, Mr. Grey. Hello, Mr. Richards. Would you care to come aboard?"

CHAPTER 6

THE waterfront was deserted; a foot-long gutting knife hung loose from the Italian's belt, and the girl with her long slim legs and her smile had the look of the classic decoy.

"We'd very much like to talk to you"—it was Peter who found his voice first—"but in *our* house rather than yours."

The man in the red-striped jersey muttered quietly in Italian, and a fisherman climbed out of the wheelhouse and picked his way aft, getting into a position from which, if he jumped ashore, he would be between Peter and Ken and their ship.

The girl smiled, tongue-between-teeth. "I'm not sure," she said, "that I'd feel safe in *your* house!"

Ken was watching the fisherman. His arm nudged Peter's. "We'd best be getting back."

They departed with far more haste than courtesy, fully expecting the man in the stern to try and block their retreat. But he didn't move. When they were safely past him, Peter glanced back. The red-jerseyed skipper, he thought, looked angry, and the girl—much to his annoyance—amused.

They didn't go to the market; for they had other things to think of than buying vegetables.

It seemed to Ken, as they discussed this latest development in Malloy's cabin, that the facts allowed of only one interpretation. The girl had been spying on them at Lob's Wood, she had been with the men who had beaten him up in his flat, now she was with the fishermen who were tailing them. Obviously she, and the Italians in the trawler, were members of the Mafia working for Schultz.

Peter wasn't so sure: "She may have saved your life, you know, getting you to Saint Thomas's. And she doesn't *look* like one of the Mafia."

"How do *you* know what the Mafia look like?"

He hadn't an answer to that; but he was not convinced.

They agreed to tighten up on security—never going ashore unless they were armed, keeping *Oyster*'s engines at instant readiness, and under no circumstances letting anyone alongside. Not that they expected trouble for the time being; for they thought it unlikely that the Mafia would show their hand until the treasure was located, if not raised.

The next few days were the most frustrating of their lives.

Friday: and the *ghibli* still moaning in from the desert and *Oyster* confined to harbour.

Saturday: and the *ghibli* dying but the sea too rough for towing the magnetometer.

Sunday: six hours uneventful towing watched by the trawler.

Monday: ten hours of uneventful towing watched by a pair of sponge divers.

Tuesday: a kick from the magnetometer, *Pearl* lowered posthaste to the bed of the sea, expectation as the divers hacked away with their mattocks at a mound in the sand, then disillusion as they laid bare not the Rommel treasure but a rusty and defused mine.

Wednesday: ten hours of uneventful towing; the area more

than half-combed, and the doubts that had been lying fallow at the back of their minds beginning to put out root.

But late on Thursday, as they were almost giving up hope, they got the breakthrough.

The day had been still, windless and uneventful, and they were about to resign themselves to another fruitless series of runs when late in the afternoon the needle of the magnetometer gave a sudden kick. Then a series of kicks in quick succession, all within a radius of twenty to thirty yards. They cast round in widening circles and picked up six recordings, one much stronger than the rest.

Ken's eyes were bright with excitement. "Could be the lifeboat and crates!"

"Could be another clutch of mines!" Malloy turned to the skipper. "Heave to and lower the cameras."

They dropped anchor above the area of maximum kick. They let down the cameras and the mercury arc lamps. They waited in an agony of hope for the screen to adjust. Then, as the representation of the seabed came flickering over the television, Ken gave a cry of elation.

For this was no false alarm.

This was it.

The picture that came welling on to the screen was too explicit for its evidence to be doubted. Five barrowlike mounds in the coarse dun sand, with the metal edge of a case protruding from one of them like a rock out of snow. The cameras moved on; and there, a little to one side, was a sixth and larger mound, the keel of a lifeboat, its rusty propellers reaching up as if in supplication to the sky.

They had found the Rommel treasure.

"And once we find it"—Malloy's words came suddenly to Peter's mind—"once we find it, the rest will be easy."

But when Malloy had spoken he hadn't known that at their moment of triumph they would be tailed by the Mafia.

They were tempted to lower the capsule at once. But it

would be dark in a couple of hours; also, Peter had noticed that since they dropped anchor the sponge boat which had been shadowing them since dawn had begun to edge uncomfortably close. So they pinpointed the spot on their charts and got under way for Benghazi.

They were like schoolboys. They laughed and joked and opened champagne and drank to the raising of what they had found. They all knew in their hearts that it would be a long hard haul before the gold lay safe in the vaults of the Banque Helvétia; but they had taken the first and most difficult step, and that for the moment was happiness enough.

By six o'clock they were secured to a buoy in the outer harbour and thinking hard.

It was no use, they realized, expecting they'd be able to drop anchor above the treasure in broad daylight, salvage it without interruption and sail it without interference to Malta. On the other hand, they wanted desperately to make at least a preliminary descent to be sure that the gold was there. This, Malloy estimated, they could do in a couple of hours. "Suppose," he said, "we douse lights and slip away during the night?"

Ken shook his head. "I reckon they'll be watching for that."

"Couldn't we fool them by transferring our riding lights to the dinghy? And leaving it behind on a buoy?"

It was an idea to work on; and a little after seven o'clock they moved *Oyster* to a new berth by the wall of the commercial basin. This, when the waterfront arcs were switched off at midnight, would be the darkest part of the harbour, and from here with the help of a little subterfuge they hoped to slip away undetected in the small hours.

At Malloy's suggestion those working at adapting the riding lights kept well out of sight, while the rest of the crew behaved ostensibly as normal: some bedded down early;

some played poker in the working space aft and some went ashore.

One of the latter was Peter. He wouldn't, he said, be ashore for long; he simply intended to buy a couple of postcards to send to his family.

It was a lovely evening as he stepped on to the quay by the Yacht Club: a full moon, the rustle of crickets and the city aglow with light. He couldn't see any danger in slipping ashore, for he had a short-barrelled Colt in his hip pocket, *Oyster* wouldn't be sailing till well after midnight, and he only wanted to go as far as the Berenice Hotel, some couple of hundred yards down the quay.

He bought his postcards in the foyer of the hotel, and took them on to the terrace which looked out over the harbour. As he settled down to write, a little Arab shoe boy—not much older than Wendy—came up with brushes, footrest and polish; but he waved him away. He selected a view of the twin-domed cathedral: "This building," he wrote to Anne, "is known locally as Mae West: for two very obvious reasons . . ."

He was addressing his last card, when some instinct made him look up.

A familiar figure was threading her way towards him between the close-packed tables: the girl from the trawler.

"Hello there, Mr. Grey!"

He got to his feet reluctantly. "Hello for the third time." His immediate reaction was not to get involved, to post his letters and beat a tragic retreat to *Oyster*. But she laid a hand on the empty chair at his table. "May I?"

Her smile was friendly and without guile.

He hesitated. He could hardly, he told himself, come to any harm talking to a girl on the crowded terrace of a very respectable hotel; and it was a chance to find out something about her, and, if she *was* mixed up with the Mafia, something about her plans. He drew back the chair.

"Thank you," her eyes were mocking. "You feel more safe with me perhaps in a hotel than a fishing boat?"

He shrugged. "They say two's company."

She shook loose her hair. She was, he decided, one of the very few girls who, seen close to, looked more beautiful rather than less. But he had no intention of being swept off his feet by her physical charms. "Do you," he asked politely, "prefer the Berenice to Lob's Wood?"

"But of course. English pubs I don't greatly care for. Such a smell of beer, and so many people."

"But quite good coffee."

She shrugged. "There are places here"—she gestured towards the city—"where you can get better coffee."

He had visions of doped *cappuccino* in a back-alley stall. "I don't doubt it! But at this time of the night you ought to be thinking of cocktails, not coffee."

Her eyes met his. "What an oblique way of offering a girl a drink."

He beckoned a waiter.

Rather to his surprise she had only bitter lemon, which she sucked through a straw like a little girl at a picnic. He decided not to beat about the bush. "What are you doing in Benghazi?"

"The same as you, I imagine."

"And what would that be?"

The blue eyes widened. "Would you wish me to be indiscreet with you, Mr. Grey? In a crowded hotel?"

Her turn of phrase—like her appearance and her very slight accent—intrigued him. "You speak sophisticated English."

"I've been to America and I studied at the Sorbonne. Paris is a very sophisticated city."

"You are French, then?"

"No. Italian."

"But of course. All the Mafia are Italian, aren't they?"

"I wouldn't know." She turned to the shoe boy who was eyeing her hopefully. *"Ciao,* Charlie!"

"Ciao, Gina. *Per favore?"*

She kicked off and handed the boy her shoes; then rather to Peter's annoyance, the two of them proceeded to converse in Italian for the better part of five minutes; and when her shoes were finished she pointed to Peter's.

"But mine are clean!"

"Please let him. I'll pay."

He put his shoe on the wooden block. "Do you get a rake-off for this?"

"No. But he needs the money."

"He'll probably blow it on comics and Coke."

Her eyes widened. "Charlie's father, Mr. Grey, happens to be over seventy and blind. He used to beg. But begging's *de trop* in Libya today. So unless Charlie brings home money his father starves."

"I apologize. How much do I give him?"

"Ten piastas."

When the boy had gone he looked at her curiously. If she was putting on a good-girl act she certainly wasn't doing it by halves. "Is that your trawler, Gina, that keeps following us around?"

She laughed. "What would I want with a trawler? Do you think perhaps I am a fishwife?"

"You seemed very much at home in it the other evening."

"The trawler, Mr. Grey, was hired by my brother. He and I are on a holiday."

"And you and your brother spend your holiday fishing off Benghazi. I suppose for mullet?"

She made a rude noise through the end of her straw. "So many questions before dinner, what *will* you be asking after!"

He stared at her, undecided, then glanced at his watch. "Join me, and find out."

It was her turn now to look at him curiously. "Why do you wish to have dinner with me?"

"Why does a man usually invite a pretty girl to dinner?"

For a moment she hesitated, then she smiled. "I suppose," she said, "for ulterior motives." She pushed back her chair and walked through the folding doors that led to the restaurant.

It was a strange meal. They were attracted to one another —at least Peter found the girl decidedly attractive; *her* reactions, as he kept on reminding himself, were probably feigned —yet they didn't trust each other an inch, and whenever one of them turned the conversation to what was going on in the waters north of Benghazi, the other shut up like the proverbial clam. And yet Peter enjoyed himself. White-jacketed waiters, palms, a cosmopolitan crowd, good food and wine, and the prettiest girl in the room: it was the sort of challenge that he hadn't measured up to for years. After a while he stopped trying to pump the girl for information: "If you won't talk of the present, Gina, tell me about your past."

"What makes you think I've got one?"

Their eyes met. "An attractive girl like you!"

She fingered the stem of her wineglass. "You'd be bored."

"I'll risk it. Please."

"Well"—she clasped her hands in her lap, like a little girl at a party about to recite—"I was born in Brindisi during the war. My parents had an estate a few miles outside the town in the Puglia Hills. It must have been lovely fifty years ago. All marble, vines and olives and servants by the dozen. Real feudal"—he was suddenly reminded of the dream world of Suzie Wong, the waterfront prostitute, and wondered—"my father was in the Navy; he died a few months before I was born, and the estate's been crumbling slowly to bits ever since. German looting, American occupation, Communist riots. *I've* plenty of outside interests to stop me brooding about it. But it's different for Mother. Since Father died her whole life has been wrapped up in the estate: a long hopeless battle to turn back the clock. I'd give anything, absolutely *anything* to help her put it back on its feet." Her fingers, he noticed, were locked so tightly together that the knuckles were white. "But you've never," she added, "been to La Normanna. So all this can't mean very much . . . When I was nine I went to a convent. You'd be surprised what went on *there*. It was a sort of cross between those two funny English schools I've read about."

"Which are they?"

"You know. Saint Trinian's and the Passion Flower Hotel. I stayed there till I was seventeen, then I got a scholarship to the Sorbonne."

"And what did they teach you at the Sorbonne?"

She smiled at him: "A bit of English. A bit of French. When I left I got a job as a hostess with Alitalia; that was fun for a time. Then I became—how do you call it?—a girl Friday in Kentucky, in one of those fabulous olde American homesteads, full of Cadillacs, racehorses and what were once called slaves."

"Did you enjoy that?"

"I enjoyed the racehorses and Cadillacs. But I don't like feeling owned."

"So you left."

"Yes, I went for a walk. I walked all the way to Alabama: with Dr. Martin Luther King."

He looked at her with interest. "And do you suppose that did any good?"

"It did *me* a lot of good."

"Hmmm! And from Alabama you walked to Benghazi?"

"In a roundabout sort of way."

"But why of all places in the world, Benghazi?"

She hesitated; for a long time. And he suddenly got the impression that irrespective of whether everything else had been fact or fancy, she was going now to tell him the truth.

"I came to Benghazi," she said slowly, "to visit my father's grave." And before he could frame any of the half-dozen questions that sprang to his mind, she drained and held out her glass. "And now," she said, "for the story of *your* life."

He protested. *Her* story, he told her, was just getting interesting. But she was adamant. "A gentleman," she told him primly, "knows when to take no for an answer."

So he began reluctantly, to tell her of his schooldays, of his wartime flying, his marriage with Jean, the birth of their children, his work as a solicitor, his daughter's ambition to become a concert pianist, and of how his world had fallen apart five years ago in the burnt-out wreck of a car.

She was a good listener, and when he had finished her eyes were sympathetic. "But why haven't you married again?"

"That," he said, "is my affair."

She looked at him thoughtfully. "I don't believe you've slept with a woman for five years!"

He was used to frankness (some of the things his daughter came out with amazed him), but this, he thought, was going a bit far. "I didn't comment, Gina, on the number of men you have or haven't slept with."

There was an awkward silence. Then she laid a hand on his arm. "I am truly sorry if I offended you. The English, I know, are very reticent about their sex life."

She was so solemn that he had to smile. "Over reticent, I dare say . . . Coffee?"

She nodded.

On the way to the terrace he glanced at his watch. It was after ten, long past the time he had planned to return to *Oyster*. He hoped that Gina wouldn't be difficult to get rid of; he had the feeling that all her sophisticated talk of sex could well have an innuendo.

The terrace was dreamlike: the great gold moon slung like a lantern over the palms, the lap of waves on sand, and the lights of the ships in harbour reflected on an onyx sea. But as they sipped their coffee constraint began to build up between them. It was as if they were both weighing up how much the evening had meant. Soon she stubbed out her cigarette and asked what time he wanted to get aboard. It was the cue for which he had been waiting.

"About an hour ago! You'll be all right, won't you, getting home?" Whatever the reply, he had no intention of escorting her either to the trawler or to some back-alley lodging.

"Yes, thank you. I've only to climb one flight of stairs."

"You're staying here? In the Berenice?"

As she got to her feet she jingled the key of her room. "I don't know how to thank you, Mr. Grey, for the super dinner. I hope we meet again."

"If we're fishing the same waters," he said slowly, "we probably will."

She hesitated, moistened her lips, then unexpectedly, laid a hand on his arm. "Fishing off Benghazi can be dangerous. Especially after you've landed your catch."

And before he could ask what she meant, she was climbing the marble staircase to her room. He might have felt more inclined to follow, if she hadn't been quite so obvious in showing him the number on her key.

As he made his way to the Yacht Club he reflected, a little wryly, that in one respect the evening had been wasted: the girl was still an enigma and of her plans he had discovered nothing. She was attractive and diverting; but that was beside the point. She had barely bothered to conceal that she was mixed up in the search for the Rommel treasure, and whom would she be working for if not the Mafia? As for her estate, her convent and her Cadillacs, they could all too easily be dreams.

Back in *Oyster* he was received with disapproval. "Where the hell have *you* been?" Ken's voice was sharp with anxiety. "We've been worried stiff."

"I met our girl friend from the trawler."

"We know that. We had our binoculars on you."

He wasn't amused. And yet he could understand how they felt. He had said he was going to post a couple of letters, and it must seem to those aboard that he had chosen a perverse moment to flirt with danger. "I only wanted," he grunted, "to find out her plans."

"And did you?"

He told Ken what had happened. For a while his observer was silent, puffing away at his pipe, then he said slowly, "If you *had* gone to her room I reckon you'd have been kidnapped by the Mafia. And held to ransom."

"It's possible."

"It's about the oldest trick in the world! Anyhow, you're back in one piece . . . You want to see how we've rigged the lights?"

Most of the crew had dossed down early; but Peter and Ken, too excited to sleep, stayed on deck, willing the moonlight and the night life to subside. It was a slow process. At eleven o'clock Benghazi's streets and waterfront were still ablaze with light and full of traders and pleasure seekers; but by midnight the lights had coalesced into little clusters around the nightclubs and bars, the harbour arcs were switched off, and the crowds had thinned; while by one o'clock city and harbour lay dark and silent under the moon. Soon, as flecks of cloud came drifting in from the desert, even the moonlight lost its power. And Benghazi slept.

They woke the crew. Each man had been carefully briefed and knew exactly what to do. There was no need for orders as they padded barefoot over the dew-wet decks, casting off ropes that had been specially greased, and easing their riding lights on to the dinghy's mast. A nod from McArthur, and quiet as a ghost ship, *Oyster* inched clear of her moorings, leaving behind on her dinghy a cluster of lights that would have satisfied all but the most suspicious of watchers. They edged quietly along the wall of the commercial basin, hugging the shadows and avoiding the beam of the pierhead light.

They thought they had made it; for there was no sign of movement from the sponge boats and trawler which, for the past ten days, had been attendant as shadows. But they were taking no chances. Even in the open sea they didn't increase speed for fear of the deeper throb of their engines and the telltale white of their bow wave; nor did they show lights, but mounted a round-the-compass watch. And there was no visible sign that they were being followed.

But being followed they were. And after a while they knew it. For when the operator tuned up his radar set, he cursed. Two pear-shaped blips were creeping on to the screen: blips which, from a range of a couple of miles, followed their every alteration of course.

From *Oyster*'s deck they could see nothing. But they knew they were not alone. Their subterfuge had been seen through. The trawler and sponge boats had not been as somnolent as they looked.

CHAPTER 7

THE moment of danger, they realized, would be when they were searching the seabed for the crates—for with *Pearl* suspended over their stern by chains and airlines they wouldn't be able to use their speed to avoid being boarded. So they had, somehow, to shake their pursuers off, if only for a couple of hours.

It was Ken who came up with the idea; not especially original or clever, but the best they could think of. "Why don't we," he suggested, "drop anchor close to the wreck of the *Selina* and kid them we think the treasure's *there?* We could put down a diver to make it realistic and spend the morning testing equipment. Then in the afternoon we could up-anchor and move off along the coast in the direction of Tobruk. Whoever is shadowing us will follow and be drawn away from the search area. By the time it's dark we could be forty or fifty miles from Benghazi; and then we could step on the gas, shake the shadowers off and cut back for a couple of hours' diving. And when the others *do* come racing after us, with any luck they'll make for the wreck."

There were plenty of ifs and buts, but the idea seemed worth a try. So they altered course for the *Selina.*

As the stars lost their brilliance and the sky in the east flushed pink, they made dummy runs round the wreck of the merchantman. And after a couple of hours, as if they had found what they were looking for, they hove to.

The sponge boats also hove to.

At first they could only see their reflections, aglint on the screen of the radar; but as the sun rose the vessels themselves came into view, hull down on the horizon. And after a while they closed in. They made not the slightest pretence now of diving for sponges, but watched *Oyster* quite openly through binoculars.

Malloy made a great show of swinging out the capsule, putting a safety diver into the sea, and testing cameras, suction pumps and every possible item of equipment—taking care the while that they had plenty of time to get away should the sponge boats think of making a run at them. But the sponge boats, it seemed, were happy to keep their distance and watch.

It was coming up to midday when their radar picked up another echo heading directly towards them from the direction of Benghazi. They guessed what vessel it would be even before the spars and booms of the trawler appeared over the horizon. They expected her to drop anchor beside the spongers. But she didn't. She kept coming on: fast, and straight toward them.

Peter's fingers beat a tattoo on the rail. "She won't try boarding us. In broad daylight."

Malloy was inclined to agree. But he was taking no chances. He picked up a megaphone. He unlocked the gun room and handed round the Winchester 300s. "Mr. McArthur, if she disregards a warning, fire a single shot into her hull."

They waited, gripping their rifles, feeling unreal as the cast of a melodramatic film. This sort of thing, they told themselves, couldn't really be happening, in the twentieth century, and to them!

When the range was down to a hundred yards, Malloy raised his megaphone. And the trawler, as if at a signal, swung to one side and reduced speed. As she came abeam, a bikini-clad figure climbed on to the roof of her wheelhouse and waved. It was Gina. Her voice came to them clearly over the sunlit water. "Hello, Mr. Grey! How's fishing?"

"Very promising."

"I don't believe you. You won't find anything here."

Malloy looked thoughtfully at Peter. "Your girl friend," he said, "knows altogether too much."

As the trawler drew slowly ahead of them they noticed she had an unusual item of equipment stowed in the lee of her fo'c'sle: a small speedboat. She didn't go far, but dropped anchor about half a mile on their port bow. They were pretty well encircled now, by the sponge boats inshore and the trawler to seaward.

Malloy turned to the skipper. "Are you ready to weigh anchor?"

"The moment you say."

"Well, don't wait for an order. The moment one of those boats moves an inch towards us, up-anchor and run."

They kept their engines idling and had lunch brought out to the working area aft.

While they ate, the lookout in the crow's nest kept up a running commentary on the other boats' movements . . . "The sponge divers' crews are an idle lot—they're simply loafing on deck—but the trawler's are hoppin' about like a nest of ants. They're lowering nets; trying to kid us, I suppose, they're sardine fishers. Now they're hoisting out the speedboat—it's a classy-looking bit of work, I must say. Now the girl is getting into it—she's a classy bit of work too! She's got some sort of apparatus with her, could be water skis." A pause; then, "I reckon we're going to have an exhibition." Another pause. "Hmmm! And very nice too!"

Peter drank the last of his Mineralé and walked to the rail.

The speedboat, with the girl in tow, was circling *Oyster*; and her circles, he noticed after a while, were contracting.

He wasn't sure what Gina was up to: was she showing off, or trying to get a closer look at the capsule? Neither motive appealed to him; but he had to admit that she was well worth watching. She was wearing a fawn-coloured bathing cap and a fawn bikini, and with her hair covered and her body suntanned she looked as if she was naked. He didn't know much about water skiing, except that it *could* be dangerous; and each time she swung over the speeedboat's wake, the breath caught in his throat. As the boat cut close under *Oyster*'s bow she switched the tow rope to her right hand and waved.

They watched her in silence. It was Malloy who suddenly cottoned on to what she was planning. "Joe!"—he grabbed the nearest diver by the arm—"See she doesn't get aboard."

The words were hardly out of his mouth, when she let go of the tow rope and came gracefully alongside, reaching out for the ladder which the safety diver had left dangling over their quarter.

Malloy leaned over the rail. "Sorry, lady. No visitors."

She had one foot on the bottom rung of the ladder. She seemed to be having difficulty with one of her skis. For a second she ducked underwater, groping for the release catch; then she bobbed up, took off her bathing cap, shook loose her hair and started to climb the ladder.

"I said no visitors." Malloy's voice was sharp.

She hesitated. She looked at Peter, and he shook his head. She looked at Joe Blair who was squatting at the top of the ladder, and the fifteen-stone ex-Marine put up his hand. "One more step, little mermaid, and I'll be obliged to toss you right back into the water!"

She smiled at him sweetly. "You and who else?" She came hand over hand up the ladder.

It happened in a good deal less time than it takes to tell. He put the flat of his hand on her shoulder—he didn't, he told them afterwards, intend to hurt her, just to be sure that she didn't climb any higher—but she was covered in suntan oil and his hand slipped from shoulder to breast. Before he knew what was happening she got a judo lock on his wrist, leaned back and heaved him neatly over her head.

His reaction was instinctive. As he fell, his legs wrapped in a scissors hold round her neck. If she hadn't let go of the ladder she would have been killed.

They fell side by side into the sea with an almighty splash. It would be hard to say who was more shaken. Blair grabbed the ladder, spitting water. "Hey there! You all right?"

She trod water, swearing at him with a fluency that transcended the language barrier. She waved to the man in the speedboat, and he came sweeping up in a cloud of spray and hauled her aboard. She was, Peter was glad to see, more angry than hurt. She jumped to her feet, nearly capsizing the speedboat, and let fly another broadside of vitriolic Italian.

Ken covered his ears. "That girl," he said, "was never brought up in a convent!"

As the speedboat carried her, angrily rubbing her neck, back to the trawler, Joe Blair came slowly up the ladder, and he was rubbing his wrist. "Just my luck," he muttered, "a mermaid that knows her judo!"

They laughed; but the incident might have had an ending that was anything but funny, and they were thankful that the next few hours were uneventful—uneventful and somnolent, as the ships swung sun-drenched and idle against their anchors.

It was siesta time; and even the gulls were motionless, asleep in the midday haze.

It was *Oyster* who broke the spell. In midafternoon she

suddenly hauled in capsule and divers and stood northeast for Tobruk.

The sponge boats hadn't expected this. Men appeared on their decks with binoculars, and there was much to-ing and fro-ing between fo'c'sle and bridge. Then, after obvious hesitation, they too hauled in their anchors, and the three vessels moved off in a ragged procession. The trawler, rather to their surprise, made no attempt to keep up with them.

All afternoon the little armada ran parallel to the Barce escarpment. They could tell that the sponge boats were puzzled—whenever *Oyster* altered course or speed binoculars focussed on her suspiciously—but having made up their minds to follow, they clung close to either quarter. After a couple of hours, by which time they were nearing Tocra, Malloy decided to see how difficult it was going to be to shake them off. Imperceptibly he increased speed. The spongers had no apparent difficulty in maintaining eight or even ten knots; but at speeds over twelve knots they began to make smoke and to drop astern. It was what they had hoped; and as the sun dipped seaward Malloy and McArthur got together in the chart room to work out a detailed plot.

It was exactly six-thirty as *Oyster* increased to maximum speed and swung suddenly into the sunset.

They were more than forty miles now from the search area. And the sponge boats were in trouble. One of them gave up at once and disappeared into the inshore haze belching smoke; the other made a brief attempt to follow them out to sea, but it wasn't long before she too disappeared under the horizon.

At over twenty knots they headed back for Benghazi. Alone. So far so good. But for the second time that day when they switched on their radar, they got an extremely unpleasant surprise. For the screen was speckled with interference.

The operator couldn't make it out. The set had been

working perfectly all morning; but it was now so badly pockmarked that it was difficult to see how far their pursuers were falling behind. They could only hope it would be working better by the time they dropped anchor above the treasure.

As they raced through waters now darkening from sapphire to indigo, they drew lots to see who should make the descent—for with Sam Mearns still struggling with a cold and Joe Blair with a sprained wrist, they were short of divers. Malloy was thankful he had insisted the whole crew make as many practice descents as possible—in the ten days they had been at Benghazi they had averaged nearly a descent a day—so that any one of them now would feel reasonably at home at a depth of three hundred feet. He asked for volunteers to go down with the senior diver. The volunteers put their names in a hat. And the name drawn out was Peter's.

An hour later, briefed, equipped and on tenterhooks, Peter and Grindly clambered in through the air locks at the bottom of the capsule.

Inside there was barely room for the two of them to sit in comfort, for the interior was cluttered with depth gauges, emergency breathing apparatus, carbon dioxide indicators and instruments for measuring their proportion of oxygen and helium. It was claustrophobic; like being immured in a nightmare coffin. The air locks were closed. And as the levers sighed into position Peter's mouth felt suddenly dry; for they were now sealed off from the rest of the world as effectively as cosmonauts about to be launched into space.

The voice of the doctor came booming through the loudspeaker, thrown back as in a science fiction fantasy by the circular walls of the capsule. "I'm raising the pressure slowly to thirty feet." Their eardrums pricked, and the needle of the pressure gauge crept to double that of the atmosphere.

"Carbon dioxide content?"

"Nought point two-five."

"Emergency cylinders?"

"Four bottles full."

"Right. Equalize your eardrums and I'll get cracking on changing the air."

They leaned back, breathing deeply, their bodies becoming gradually acclimatized to the increasing pressure and their lungs to the increasingly dense mixture of oxy-helium; while in the world they had already to all intents and purposes left behind them, *Oyster*, with lights doused, moved slowly into position above the treasure. They couldn't see much through the single porthole: just the occasional shadow moving over the darkened deck as television cameras, loud-hailer, suction pump and arc lamps were swung into position over the rails. Then the deck plates stopped vibrating, and they knew that *Oyster* had hove to.

It was the moment they had worked for and dreamed of.

A slight jerk, a rattling of chains and they felt themselves hoist into the air. A splash as they entered the water, and against the porthole the grey of night gave way to the indigo of sea. Peter stared into the darkness, too intrigued to be afraid; he could see nothing and feel nothing, but he could hear the rattling of chains and the hissing intake of oxy-helium. After about half a minute the rattling stopped, and the voice of the doctor came booming over the intercom. "We've steadied you at thirty feet. We're checking the capsule for leaks."

They hung suspended in the alien sea, their only links with life the metal chain that bound them to *Oyster* and the fragile and gently swaying air lines.

A light flared up beside the capsule, a light so bright that Peter involuntarily raised a hand to his eyes. He thought for a moment there had been an explosion; then he realized it was only the mercury arc lamp, which from now on would spotlight their every move and relay it to the watchers on *Oyster*'s deck.

Into the light of the arc swam a frogman: black, grotesque and obscurely evil. It was a relief to recognize under the Frankenstein mask the face of big Joe Blair. He moved slowly round the capsule, checking for leaks. When he found no sign of the telltale bubbles, he tapped on the porthole, making a circle with his thumb and forefinger (the international divers' sign for O.K.). A pause. Then the chains resumed their rattling and the oxy-helium its hissing, and they were lowered down, down and everlastingly down in a pool of light which seemed to increase in brilliance as the water around them grew darker.

They stared at the indicators, equalizing the pressure in their ears.

As they descended, the pressure increased and the proportion of oxygen that was fed into the capsule was progressively reduced to no more than seven per cent. The depth gauge unwound slowly: one hundred feet, two hundred, three hundred. At three hundred and ten feet the rattle of cables stopped. Everything was suddenly very quiet. And looking out they could see a little below them the bed of the Mediterranean: a circle of coarse gold sand illuminated by the light of the arc. They didn't speak—one of the peculiarities of oxy-helium is that it reduces the human voice to an unrecognizable squawk—but the senior diver pointed to the air lock, and Peter gave him the O.K.

They unbolted the hatches: first the inner, then the outer. And as the doors swung open Peter could feel the sweat prick up on his palms. For this was the moment of truth. If there was the slightest defect in their equipment or the slightest impurity in the mixture they were breathing, they would now have only seconds to live—and what seconds, as they fought in agony for breath.

They put on masks and hookah-type breathing tubes. They lowered themselves through the hatchway and on to the bed of the sea and found they could breathe and move as easily as if they were only a few feet under the surface.

Peter's first reaction was relief still to be alive. But as he looked about him his relief gave way to loneliness and an indefinable fear. This wasn't the world he knew. This was a world as strange and alien as the farther face of the moon. It was the light that troubled him most. His field of vision was far less than he had expected. Within a twenty-foot radius of the arc lamp everything stood out clearly: the capsule itself aglow as if outlined in phosphorous, sea anemones of unbelievable brilliance, and shoals of little red-gold fish that flitted like fireflies through the water. But beyond the light of the arc the world tailed off into Stygian darkness: a darkness full of terrors all the greater for being so close and yet unseen.

"Hi there! We're watching you!" Malloy's voice was about the most welcome sound he had ever heard. He waved at the cameras, and felt less frightened and alone.

"We can't see the crates on the screen"—this was Malloy again. "You must have drifted off course in the descent."

It was for just this eventuality that they had brought the magnetometer, and the senior diver was already unlashing it from the side of the capsule: not the magnetometer they had used from the surface, but an underwater adaptation which looked like a cross between a mine detector and a vacuum cleaner. This he pushed in front of him, while Peter swam by his side with a pressurized torch.

If they had been operating by day in shallow water they could have seen the lifeboat and crates at once; but by night at three hundred feet they had to search for them. But they knew they couldn't be far. They swam side by side into the darkness, the diver moving his detector slowly over the sand, and Peter checking back every few seconds to see that the air lines were running free. Each time they breathed out a little skein of bubbles floated upward, nosed at by inquisitive fish. Most of the fish were tiny; but once a grouper, all of three feet long, came darting into the beam of the torch. Peter was so startled that he caught his breath, half choked, and blundered into the diver. It took them nearly a minute to disentangle their lines.

They had gone less than a dozen yards from the capsule when the needle kicked. It kicked again and again. And when they shone their torch on the spot where it kicked most strongly, they spotlit a rise in the seabed and the rusty curve of a propeller protruding out of a mound of sand.

Clumsy with excitement, they scooped away with their mattocks. Almost at once they hit metal. And within seconds they were laying bare the hull of a lifeboat.

It never occurred to them to doubt it was the *Selina*'s. And yet, as the sand was laboriously mattocked away, there was no mistaking the letters that began to stand out one by one on the battered stern: first a P, then an O, then an L and finally an I. For a moment they stared at each other, disbelieving, then they returned to the attack with renewed vigour, the force of their blows rebounding them slow and weightless to a distance of several feet and stirring up an opaque gyration of sand. But at last they uncovered the whole of the stern plaque: *Selina: Napoli.*

They couldn't talk. But they hugged each other with squeaks of delight and swam back to pass the good news to the others. Malloy seemed to sense their jubiliation as they came swimming into the circle of arc light. "Hi, there! Have you found the treasure?"

Three flashes on the torch for no.

"The lifeboat?"

One flash for yes.

"Good for you!" The words were trite; but their warmth came down to them through three hundred feet of sea. "You must be just about treading on the cases. You O.K. to stay down?"

The senior diver looked at Peter, who nodded.

"Right. You've been down thirty-five minutes. We'll give you another thirty-five. If we want you back sooner—say there's an emergency—we'll toll the ship's bell over the intercom. O.K.?"

They circled thumb and forefinger to the cameras and began to make parallel runs with the magnetometer, knowing that within a very few yards lay treasure enough to make them millionaires.

And they found it almost at once.

Only a few feet outside the circle of arc light the magnetometer kicked, not so strongly this time, but a definite recording. And there, spotlit in the beam of Peter's torch, was a smooth little hummock of sand.

They hacked at it eagerly—too eagerly to start with, the impetus of their blows drifting them off in the unresisting sea and raising a miniature *ghibli.* They forced themselves to dig slowly and carefully, and after a while they hit metal. Atap with their mattocks they traced the outline of what they had found: a black metal case, exactly the size of the cases that Peter had last seen twenty-five years ago in the waterlogged sheets of the lifeboat. It took them nearly ten minutes to prise off the lid: ten frustrating minutes as their mattocks, cushioned by water, slithered off the tough steel plates and the sea grew opaque with churned-up sand. But at last one of the hinges caved in, and they got a crevice on which to purchase. They tore off the lid; and there in the beam of their torch lay tier after tier of twelve-inch by four-inch bars of a dark lackluster metal, neatly stacked, like elongated bricks.

They levered one of them out. They peered at it in an agony of doubt. It didn't *look* like gold; it was the right consistency and weight but the wrong colour, a charcoal black unlightened by even a fleck of yellow.

The diver pulled out his knife and began, delicately as a

surgeon, to scrape away at the outer skin. And there suddenly took place the most wonderful metamorphosis as the tarnish pared off, revealing, like a butterfly in its chrysalis, the unmistakable glitter of gold.

They had found it. But for a moment they didn't dare to believe that here at their feet lay the desideratum of so many dreams. As if in a daze they loaded two or three bars as samples into a small net, then they swam the few yards to another crate, which Peter had spotted rising darkly out of the sand.

They were starting to prise the second case open, when the silence was split by a crescendo of sound: the pealing of *Oyster*'s bell.

They froze, fear welling up in them like blood from a cut. They grabbed the magnetometer and the net and struck out fast for the capsule.

As they came threshing into the circle of arc light the cameras and suction pump were already being hauled in, and Malloy's voice had the edge of panic. "Into the capsule. Quick."

It was no time for questions. They slithered in through the air lock, slammed the hatches, and flashed the light to indicate they were ready to be winched in. And the capsule at once jerked off the bed of the sea to a squealing cacophony of chains.

They looked at each other, wondering. Then the calm unhurried voice of the doctor drowned the jangle of the winch. "You're coming up fast, so don't try adjusting the pressure. . ." A pause, then: "Just to put you in the picture, we've picked up three ships that seem to be homing on us. With interference on the screen, they got pretty close before we spotted them. But they're *our* worry. You just sit tight and enjoy the ride!"

They sat tight, but they didn't enjoy the ride. They stared at the depth gauge, moistening their lips and shivering with cold as the water about them grew paler. They thought at first that they were coming up in a single run; but at a depth of just under eighty feet the clatter of cables died, the capsule jerked to a stop, and they hung motionless in a silence so absolute they could hear the sigh of the oxy-helium flowing in through the tubes.

"Why the hell have we stopped?" was what Peter *wanted* to say, but all that came out of his throat was a mouselike cheep.

The senior diver, however, seemed to understand; he reached for his pad. *I expect,* he wrote, *they'll test for leaks before they hoist us aboard.*

But the senior diver was wrong.

For a couple of minutes they hung motionless in chains; then a shadow moved dark over the porthole: the shadow of a frogman. They thought it was big Joe Blair, checking for air bubbles. Then the frogman came closer and pressed his face to the porthole, and his face was the face of a stranger.

For a moment the three of them, cut off from the rest of the world, stared at one another unwinking. Then the frogman moved a finger slowly across his throat.

He pulled out a knife.

He reached for their air lines.

And with a single slash cut through the rubber hose.

Their oxy-helium dried up with a sigh.

Peter would have died within seconds if the senior diver hadn't done the right thing by instinct. In a single movement he slammed the air-supply lever to closed (thus preventing loss of pressure through the severed tubes) and switched over to their emergency cylinders.

They clung to the walls of the capsule, trembling, drenched with sweat and sucking in great gulps of the lifesaving oxy-helium. Each of their emergency cylinders had sufficient mixture in it to keep one person alive for twenty or maybe twenty-five minutes, but no more.

The senior diver reached for the light switch. He was about to flash *Oyster* in Morse to haul them in, when there was a dull reverberating roar and the capsule rocked uneasily in the shock waves of an underwater explosion. The dials of their instruments flickered, and a torch fell off its hook and shattered on the deck plates.

A moment of silence, and the sweat running cold into Peter's eyes. Then two more explosions in quick succession, and the capsule jerking and quivering like an animal in pain.

They looked at each other, and the fear in their eyes was too elemental to hide: so, they knew, must the crew of a submarine have felt in the war with depth charges creeping close—only they were more vulnerable than any submarine.

All they could do was wait, wait and pray, the only movement the uneasy rock of the capsule and the only sound the rasping pant of their breath as they sucked at the tubes from the emergency cylinders. The seconds ticked by. They were beginning to wonder if the crisis—whatever the crisis might be—was over, when it happened.

A clap like thunder: a bright magnesium light, and the sea about them exploded into myriad particles of white. There was the shriek of metal, the splinter of glass and the hiss of air tubes whipping about the capsule like striking snakes. Then, quite suddenly, they were falling in absolute silence. For the chain that bound them to *Oyster* had parted.

They fell into darkness like a plane aspin through the tropopause, down and round, round and down, faster and faster towards the far-off bed of the sea.

Peter shut his eyes: please God, he whispered, look after Anne and the little ones.

They bulldozed into the sand stern-first, with the force of a meteorite. Peter's head cracked on the rim of the porthole. The last thing he saw as he lost consciousness was the emergency breathing mask, ripped off his mouth and drifting weightless into the center of the capsule. And the last thing he heard was the voice of his daughter: "Don't imagine we'll say thank you for all the gold in the damned *Selina* if anything happens to *you*."

CHAPTER 8

THE radar operator couldn't understand what had happened to his set. It had been working perfectly in the morning, but for the last few hours, it had been speckled with interference. He had tuned it and dismantled it, changed the components and reassembled and tested it, but still the great bands of interference come flooding on to his screen. The interference made it difficult to pick up and identify an echo: difficult, but not, to the trained eye, impossible.

It was a few minutes after Peter and Grindly had been lowered to the bed of the sea that an idea which had been forming for some time in the operator's mind took definite shape. He flicked off the tuning control and walked thoughtfully to the bridge. "Gary!"

"Hmmm?"

"You know what *could* be the trouble."

Malloy, immersed in calculations, gave the operator only half his attention. "What's that?"

"A homing aid stuck on to our hull."

"But for Christ's sake! No one's been alongside to stick one on!"

"There *has* been one person alongside."

Malloy looked up from his plot. The operator had his attention now. "Yes," he said slowly, "you're right."

"If Sam Mearns would stand by the screen, I'd like to take a look at the hull."

Ten minutes later, in swim fins and snorkel, he was lowering himself over the side.

And at about the time that the water was closing over his head, a pear-shaped blip came creeping into the bottom left-hand corner of the radar screen. The operator, being an expert, would have identified the blip in a couple of minutes; but to Sam Mearns it was inseparable from the clutter of interference.

In his anxiety not to show too much light, the operator was using a low-powered torch, and he could only examine a small portion of the hull at a time. So it was quite a while before he found what he was looking for: the miniature homer clamped like an evil excrescence on to the plates of their quarter. Only one person had had the opportunity to clamp it there: the girl from the trawler, when she had come alongside and ducked underwater ostensibly to loosen her skis. He wrenched the antenna off. He smashed the transmitter against the hull and tossed it angrily into the sea. But the damage, he knew, had been done.

He was about to heave himself back over the rail when he heard Sam Mearns's shout. "Gary! The screen's cleared. And there's something on it."

There were in fact three things on it: three pear-shaped blips, which, in the twenty-odd minutes that the operator had been away, had climbed from the corner of the screen to not very far off-center. The operator would have identified them in spite of the interference; but it wasn't until the screen cleared that Sam Mearns realized, in a moment of dismay, that they were the sponge boats and trawler.

They stared at the screen, for a moment mesmerized to

inaction by the inching forward of the blips. Ill luck and a touch of carelessness had combined to bring about the very situation they wanted at all costs to avoid. For with *Pearl* on the bed of the sea they were hamstrung, vulnerable as a tethered animal to an advancing column of ants. They couldn't tow the capsule away at more than a couple of knots, and they couldn't cut her adrift without condemning Peter and Grindly to a certain and extremely unpleasant death.

It was Malloy who found his voice first. "How long till they get here?"

The operator adjusted his slide rule against the screen. "More than ten minutes. Less than fifteen."

"Get off an S.O.S. And haul in the capsule. Fast."

Reason told him that they wouldn't have time to hoist *Pearl* and get under way before the boats were alongside; but they had to try.

The bell tolled, the hailer blared, additional cranes were swung out; but it seemed an eternity to those on deck before Peter and the senior diver were ready to start the ascent.

Malloy made his way to the gun room. For the second time within twenty-four hours he passed out the long-barrelled Winchesters, though he had a sinking feeling this time that if the Mafia meant business it would take more than rifles to stop them.

Pearl was only eighty feet from the surface when they spotted the white of the approaching bow waves.

Malloy could have wept. So near to safety and yet so far. But it was too late now for weeping. "Stop the capsule." (The last thing he wanted was for *Pearl* to be mixed up in a fight —for a bullet into one of the outside air cylinders would make it explode like nitroglycerine, while a bullet into the porthole would reduce the pressure to normal, boiling the oxygen, in a matter of seconds, out of the divers' blood.) The hum of the winch and the clatter of chains faded and died, and in the sudden silence they could hear the midnight wind moaning soft in the rigging.

They waited, tense and trembling in the pale half-light of a dying moon, watching the bow waves creaming towards them, fast, one vessel some half-mile ahead of the others. Malloy suddenly remembered that their safety diver, Joe Blair, was still in the water, waiting for the capsule to surface. But he decided to leave him. He would be as safe in the sea, he thought, as on deck.

The leading vessel lost way. She made no effort to come alongside, but hove to a couple of hundred yards on their bow. Peering into the darkness they could make out her silhouette, squat and sinister, outlined against the moonlit sky. It was the trawler. The other vessels swept past her, swung one to port of *Oyster* and one to starboard, and came to rest on either quarter, threateningly close.

"We won't be the first to shoot"—Malloy's voice was as matter-of-fact as if he was taking the chair at a board meeting —"but if *they* start, we shoot to kill. Ready with the searchlight?"

McArthur nodded.

Malloy picked up a megaphone. He pointed to the bridge of the nearest sponger. "Light her up."

A great swathe of white leapt at the sponge diver, throwing her superstructure into garish relief. Malloy raised the megaphone. "We have radioed for police protection," he shouted. "Don't come any—"

The crack of a rifle: the tinkle of glass, and the bulb of their searchlight falling shattered to the deck.

They were men unaccustomed to violence, and it was only at this moment that they fully understood the stakes for which they were playing: it was the Mafia's lives or theirs.

They waited, crouching low under what little cover the superstructure provided, listening for the telltale plash of oars and watching the spongers' decks. The night was cool, but the palms of their hands were warm with little globules of sweat. They were totally unprepared for what came next.

Twin beams of light flickered white over the sea: beams of light which originated from the bridge of the trawler, fanned out on either side of the salvage ship and illuminated the frogmen. Thirty to forty frogmen: web-footed, grotesquely masked, and black as *tirailleurs* of the devil. They were in two groups, the larger to port and the smaller to starboard; they were less than fifty yards from *Oyster,* and they were closing fast. All this they saw in the first bright flash of illumination. Then to their horror, as their eyes grew accustomed to the glare, they saw something else: Joe Blair, with the frogmen closing in on him, swimming desperately for his life.

He was a powerful swimmer, but with a deep-water aqualung strapped to his back he hadn't a chance. Even as the men on *Oyster*'s deck threw up their rifles to fire, he was caught. There was a churning up of water, a flash of knives, a cry of pain, and he was gone and the only trace of his going a flurry of blood-red sea.

Malloy swore softly and viciously.

Then a fusillade of bullets smacked into the trawler's searchlights. And in the sudden darkness they could hear the splashing fins and panting breath of the approaching frogmen.

McArthur grabbed Ken by the arm. "With me, quick!"

They ran to the gun room. But someone was there before them: Fanny Farmer, the little Indonesian cook, was already dragging out a box of grenades. All three of them were breathing heavily, oblivious to the world as men under the spell of a narcotic and filled with a fierce almost sexual excitement, as though the threat to their lives was a challenge to their virility. They each grabbed a grenade, their minds quite blank to the consequences of what they were about to do.

"What's the setting?" Ken's voice was as shaking as his hands.

"Twelve seconds. Count six and throw."

They jerked out the pins. They forced themselves to count slowly. Then they lobbed the grenades in a spinning arc into the middle of the frogmen.

A shout of fear. A panic-stricken threshing at the sea. And then the holocaust.

Three thunderclaps of tortured sound: thunderclaps that brought men's hands to their ears, and echoed and re-echoed again and again like blasts from a quarry. Three columns of water: columns that leapt up, mast-high, like fountains of solid grey, and then fell back with a hissing sigh into the sea. Those at the center of the explosions were lucky: killed outright, their bodies drifted away into the night. It was those at the perimeter who suffered most, as, ruptured and broken-limbed, they flailed at the blood-soaked sea like gutted fish.

Mercifully, the way that most of the frogmen died was hidden by night and the flurry of the explosions. But by a freak chance the fate of one man was witnessed by all. For as the nearest column of water pyramided up, there on the very apex if its fountain hung the figure of a man: a puppet figure of broken limbs and screaming mouth, crucified as if for all eternity against a backdrop of uncaring stars.

McArthur felt the hair prick up on the nape of his neck. And Ken Richards, his stomach heaving, grabbed at the deck rail; his head throbbed violently and he thought he was going to faint.

The frogmen to port had been mauled too savagely to be of the slightest danger. But those to starboard remained. They trod water, hesitant. Voices whispered in the dark. Then the bulk of them turned and swam quickly back to the nearest sponger. But about half a dozen, braver or more foolish than their companions, came on.

Ken Richards heard them as he leaned, sick and dizzy,

against the rail. A great hammer was beating rhythmically at his brain, his eyes kept rolling out of focus and he half believed that he was back in the private wards of Saint Thomas's. Only half conscious of what he was doing, he reached for another grenade. He pulled out the pin. But before he could throw it, the Mafia were over the side: a cluster of sea-wet figures silhouetted against the horizon. He saw one of them jerk back his arm. He sensed rather than saw the flash of a knife. He swayed aside. And the knife missed his heart, nicked the very top of his shoulder and pinned him by his jacket to the door of the galley.

He hung there, splayed out like a specimen insect on a slab, while the hammer abeat at his brain built up to a wild crescendo. His eyes and his fingers opened wider and wider. And the last thing he saw, before he fainted, was his grenade rolling live into *Oyster*'s scuppers.

It was the little Indonesian cook who saved their lives. With a cry of warning he came leaping down from the roof of the galley. He didn't have time to pick the grenade up. He fly-kicked it over the side. It could, with relative safety, have landed anywhere within a dozen yards of *Oyster*'s stern; but as ill luck would have it it landed almost directly above the capsule.

There was a clap of thunder. For a moment the chain links that bound them to *Pearl* glowed incandescent in the heat of the explosion; then they parted. The tip of the chain, whipping back with a crack like an elephant whip, coiled smoking round the drum of the winch. And the capsule toppled deadweight to the bed of the sea.

They knew what had happened; but there was nothing they could do about it till they had dealt with the Mafia.

The Mafia, in fact, were dealt with easily enough.

Only six had come swarming aboard. One, in the act of climbing over the rail, had been toppled back by the blast of the explosion; another had been shot through the shoulder as he lunged at Malloy with a knife; and the others had paused irresolute. Unnerved, outnumbered and dazed with shock, they had little stomach for further violence. One raised his hands in surrender, and the rest in a panic-stricken stampede slithered back into the sea.

Within five minutes of the shot that had shattered their searchlight the attack had been beaten off. But at what a cost. The capsule lost; Joe Blair knifed savagely to death; Ken Richards pinned senseless to the door of the galley; and in the water about their hull more than a dozen of the Mafia dead or dying. They were torn between pity and fear. Their hearts pleaded with them to help the survivors; but their heads reminded them that the Mafia might still be a force to be reckoned with.

It was the trawler who solved their dilemma. A light flashed briefly from her wheelhouse and a voice hailed them in Italian. *"Si riesci a ricuperare il tuo equipaggiamento subacqueo, noi salveremo i superstiti."*

Malloy looked enquiringly at McArthur.

"I *think* he said, 'You salvage your capsule; we'll pick up the survivors.' "

Malloy's fingers drummed at the deck rail: "They're a cool lot of bastards! Tell him we agree—so long as he doesn't come near us."

McArthur reached for the megaphone: *"Accetiamo. Purchè stiate alla giusta distanza."*

"Non abbiate paura; non ci avviciveremo!" The trawler switched on her auxiliary searchlight and lowered a scrambling net. They watched her carefully as she put out a boat and began to haul the men from the water. She took no interest in what they were doing and kept a very respectful distance.

They had a lot to do and not much time in which to do it.

They realized that the capsule, chains and air lines severed, must have plummetted to the bed of the sea. They thought it unlikely that Peter and Grindly could still be alive, but if by some miracle they *were,* then every second was vital.

"McArthur"—there was no mistaking Malloy's authority in a crisis—"lock up the prisoners. And keep a watch on the trawler; if she comes within fifty yards of us, cut and run . . . Scott-Henderson"—he turned to the doctor—"never mind the fellow I shot: see to Ken . . . And you two"—he grabbed the engineer and the standby diver—"with me."

They freed the winch and the crane, which had been jammed by the backlash of the capsule's chains. They lowered arc lights, cameras and hailer—while a pair of lookouts kept an extremely watchful eye on the Mafia. But the Mafia had had the stuffing knocked out of them; and by the time that Malloy was ready to try to contact the capsule, all three vessels were drawing off in the direction of Tocra. They watched thankfully as they faded first from sight and then from the radar screen. They were rid of one anxiety, but the other and deeper anxiety remained.

"There she is!" Sam Mearns gave an excited shout as the silhouette of the cylinder came welling up on the screen. She was hovering stern-first a little above the bed of the sea; but she didn't appear to be badly damaged.

Malloy grabbed the microphone of the underwater hailer. "Hello, *Pearl.* We can see you. Are you all right?"

They waited in an agony of hope.

But there was no reply.

CHAPTER 9

THERE was a roaring in Peter's ears and a bright pulsating light in his eyes as he swam painfully back to consciousness. He thought for a moment that he was back in the Blue Lagoon, drowning, and that the boatman of the Styx was rowing towards him in his *gaiassa.* Then he realized that a mask was pressing against his mouth. Thankfully he drew in great gulps of oxy-helium, and the waters of the Styx subsided and solidified into the walls of the capsule.

The light flared out again, bright as a magnesium firework; and this time he realized what was happening. He was doubled up against the side of the capsule; the capsule, tethered by its weights, was swaying gently a couple of feet above the bed of the sea; and the light of an arc lamp was flooding in through their porthole.

"Hello, *Pearl!*" Malloy's voice came to them faintly over the hailer. "We can see you. Are you all right?"

Peter's eyes met the senior diver's; he felt his head gingerly and nodded.

Their intercom and electric leads had parted, and the glass of their torch lay white on the deck; but in the survival kit on the wall of the capsule an emergency flash lamp lay in its holder undamaged.

The arc went out. "Hello, *Pearl!* If you are all right, flash a light at the porthole."

Grindly fumbled with the lamp; he felt for the fingertip control, and a beam of light cut through the darkness and came to rest on the plates of laminated glass.

"Thank God for that!"—Malloy's usually unemotional voice was shaking. "Is the capsule airtight?"

One flash on the lamp for yes.

"Is either of you hurt?"

Three flashes for no.

"That's just fine. Check the cylinders and tell us how long your oxy-helium will last."

The senior diver looked at his watch; he checked the pressure of the unused cylinders and tested them for leaks by sucking through the mouth tubes; then his lamp flickered in Morse: "Thirty-five minutes."

"Fine again. We'll have you up long before that . . . Now I'm handing you over to the doc."

"Hello there!" Scott-Henderson's bedside manner came unimpaired through three hundred feet of sea. "Now I want you to relax: the more normally you breathe the longer your oxy-helium will last. You've nothing to worry about, because we've plenty of ideas for getting you up. We'll try the easy way first. Will one of you climb out through the air lock and see if you can release the ballast weights?"

They looked at each other. The capsule, Peter remembered, had a cluster of lead weights attached vertically beneath it to an iron bar. These worked on the same very simple principle as the weights on a diver's belt: it was only necessary to press a quick release button and the weights would drop off and the diver (or capsule), made suddenly lighter, would rise to the surface. Normally they could have shed the weights from inside *Pearl* by operating an electric motor; but with their power cut off they could only release them from the outside by hand. It would, they realized, be tricky work; for they would have to scramble back the moment the capsule started to rise, and if they didn't get in and seal up the hatches in time they would die, in the rapidly decreasing pressure, an extremely unpleasant death. But it gave them a chance. The senior diver flashed once on the lamp.

"Right, get cracking. We'll be watching you on the telly."

The air locks, mercifully, appeared to be clear of the bottom and undamaged. The senior diver put on his mask and lowered himself out of the hatch.

The metal bar into which the weights were slotted was half-buried in the sand, and while the diver scraped away at it with his mattock Peter hovered anxiously in the hatchway ready to haul him in the moment they started to rise.

But there was not the slightest sign of their rising. For the weights refused to shift.

Peter could see the diver heaving away at the release mechanism, streams of bubbles slanting out of his mask as he fought for breath. He prodded and hacked and levered and tugged, but to no avail; and after two or three minutes he came slowly back to the hatchway, weak with exhaustion. He collapsed at the entrance to the capsule, sucking in great gulps of oxy-helium. It was almost a minute before he was able to scribble a message on his pad: *Weights stuck. Come and help.*

As Peter adjusted his mask he could feel the sweat, cold and damp, beading his forehead. Already more than five of their thirty-five minutes had slid insidiously away.

As if in a nightmare, unable to speak, they worked their way under the metal hull of the capsule, bathed in the bright metallic light of the arc. They tugged and levered at the weights, while little shoals of fish paused for a moment to stare at them, glassy-eyed, then darted away into the darkness. Bubbles, rainbow-hued, streamed up to the surface. And the weights refused to move. For the bar on to which they were attached had been buckled as they plunged into the bed of the sea. Desperately they heaved and wrenched at the insensate discs of lead that stood between them and life. But the discs of lead wouldn't shift. And the minutes fled; and their breath came faster and faster until the oxy-helium was sucked clean out of their bottles, and choking and retching, they had to switch over to the last of their emergency cylinders. They knew then that they had only a little over twenty-five minutes to live.

The arc was switched off, and Scott-Henderson's voice came ghostlike out of the darkness: "Can't you move the weights?"

Three flashes for no.

A pause, then: "Get back to the capsule and rest—that'll conserve your air. We're starting to lower the spare chain for you to hook on to."

They crawled through the hatch and squatted on either side of the capsule, breathing as slowly and evenly as they could. They did their best not to look at one another. It made it worse, somehow, not being able to talk—as though a part of them was already dead—and it didn't help to know the sort of death that was now only a very few minutes away.

It seemed an eternity before the doctor's voice again came over the hailer: "The chain is halfway down. Get ready to hook it on."

They clambered out of the hatch and swam slowly to the top of the capsule. It should, Peter told himself, be comparatively easy to secure the chain to the great cast-iron hook that was riveted to the capsule's nose. But as his eyes came level with the nosecap he felt a terrible coldness seep into every pore of his body.

For the hook had been damaged beyond repair, sheared clean away by the shattering force on the chains that followed the explosion.

He was seized by a sudden determination. Everything was against them. They hadn't, according to the book, a hope in hell. But he wouldn't give up. Somehow, somewhere there must be a way out.

The senior diver had been guiding down the thick metal links of the chain as they uncoiled into the circle of arc light, and it was some minutes before he saw the damage to the hook. But he saw it now. He half-choked, the oxy-helium bubbled out of his lungs and he sank to the bed of the sea, scrabbling in impotent despair at the sand.

Peter swam down to him. He shook him angrily by the shoulder. "Don't sit there on your arse! Get up and help me tie the chain round the capsule." The words came out as a meaningless squeak, but the message got through.

"Hi there!" This was Scott-Henderson's voice on the loud-hailer. "Is something wrong with your air?"

Peter flashed three times on the lamp.

"We can't see you too well on the screen. Is the hook damaged?"

One flash for yes.

A shocked silence.

Peter could visualize the scene on *Oyster*'s deck: the hurried consultations, the time checks, the slow metamorphosis from anxiety to despair. He didn't *really* believe they'd be able to tie the chain sufficiently securely to hold the capsule in place while it was winched up. But at least it was worth a try. And the engineer controlling the cranes, realizing what they were trying to do, brought the arc lamp lower and closer to give them light.

"Take it easy," the doctor's voice boomed over the hailer. "You can't afford a mistake."

It was hard to force themselves to work slowly: hard to stop themselves panting for breath as they passed the chain under and round the capsule; and hard not to count the minutes as they slipped silently away. Was it, Peter wondered, imagination, or was there already the first faint whisper of pain from his arms and legs, as, under a pressure ten times that of the atmosphere, oxygen poisoning began to build up in his blood? He forced himself to concentrate on slipknotting the chain round the capsule, tying the knot so that when it pulled taut it would be held in place by the flanges under the porthole.

Scott-Henderson was watching them carefully. "That looks fine. Swim clear, and we'll give her a hoist."

The winch hummed; the chain tautened; the slipknot ran tight under the porthole, and to the grate and squeal of link against link the capsule was jerked away from the bed of the sea. For a moment she swayed from side to side; then she came to rest upright, mercifully steady, poised for the ascent.

"Well done!" They could sense the doctor's jubilation. "Seal yourselves in, flash when you're ready, and we'll have you up in a couple of shakes!"

They swam into the capsule. They closed the air locks and flashed the lamp. There was a moment of silence as they waited, moistening their lips and hardly daring to breathe. Then came the most wonderful sound they had ever heard: the steady rhythmic hum of the crane as it hauled them slowly up, foot by foot, out of the valley of shadow and into light. And all the while the chain held steady, with not the slightest hint of a slip.

Peter glanced at his watch. They still had sufficient oxy-helium for nearly ten minutes; the ascent would take no more than five minutes and the transfer to the decompression chamber maybe three or four, and they had as a reserve the air inside the capsule—although this was becoming increasingly contaminated by carbon dioxide. It began to look as though, against all the odds, they were going to make it. They watched the unwinding of the depth recorder: two hundred and fifty feet, two hundred feet, one hundred and fifty feet; soon they were two-thirds of the way to the surface.

"Don't try to reduce your pressure," the doctor's voice was relaxed and confident. "We'll cope with all that on deck."

They smiled at each other, conscious of the comradeship of men who have been face to face with death. Looking out through the porthole they could see the arc lights and cameras keeping pace with their ascent, and the occasional fish peering in at them through the laminated glass, while the water every second grew clearer and lighter. Soon they had less than fifty feet to go, and the capsule was swaying gently in the slight underwater swell.

It was the swell that did it. There was a sudden scraping across the plates of their hull. The capsule slewed sideways. And the chain, taut as a bowstring, began to slide in little agonized jerks across the face of the porthole.

They stared at it in horror, the hair pricking up on their scalps. For the chain that a moment ago had looked so secure was now slipping fast.

And there was nothing they could do to stop it. They could only watch, waiting in terror for the sickening plunge that would topple them back to the bed of the sea. The steel links ground slowly over the glass; they didn't move rhythmically, but in reluctant unco-ordinated jerks, as the capsule swayed this way and that in the swell.

Al Grindly leapt to his feet. He clawed at the porthole, hammering at the glass, stabbing with his finger at the gradually disappearing chain. Peter thought for a moment that he had gone off his head with fear. Then he realized what he was doing: trying to attract the attention of whoever was watching the screen.

"Take it easy, Al," the doctor's voice was infuriatingly calm, "another minute and we'll have you aboard."

The last few links of chain hung for a second, poised agonizingly on the very lip of the flange, then slid slowly back to the glass. But the capsule slewed even further sideways, and they knew that on the next roll the chain would fall free.

A muffled shout on the hailer: "Hold it!" and the capsule quivered to a stop. A pause, then the voice of the doctor: "We can't see you too well. Is the chain slipping?"

One flash for yes.

"Keep dead still. Divers are on the way down."

They hung by a thread in an alien world, helpless as a spaceship that has run out of orbit. The sea, the refracted light of the stars and the familiar outline of *Oyster*'s hull were less than fifty feet above their heads; but they might as well have been in a different world. They moved from side to side of the capsule, trying to counteract the swell, staring mesmerized at the handful of links whose movement held the key to their lives.

Now that the capsule was motionless, the chain wasn't slipping so fast; but it was still working link by straining link up to the very edge of the porthole. They could see the whole of the loop now that was holding them in place: about a dozen links slipping and slithering one by one over the glass. Ten links, nine links, eight links, seven links . . . in a matter of seconds there wouldn't be any links left and they would be plummetting to certain death.

A swirl of black and a diver peering in through the porthole. It was Sam Mearns. He gave them the thumbs up, grabbed the chain and tried to haul it back over the porthole; but the chain was too heavy for him. Another diver came down in a skein of bubbles (Malloy himself) and he too grabbed at the straining links. Peter could see little beads of perspiration running damp down the divers' faces inside their masks and the multicoloured air bubbles streaming up from their mouthpieces as they wrestled with the chain; while from under his feet came the grating rasp of a hacksaw —another diver, he realized, was trying to cut off the ballast weights.

There was a sudden bubbling in Grindly's mouth, and he was sucking in the last of his oxy-helium. Slowly he took off his mask. There was nothing he could breathe now except for the air inside the capsule. Peter passed him his mouth-piece. For a moment Grindly sucked at it greedily; then it too dried up with a sigh.

It hardly seemed to matter now that the divers were losing their battle to hold the chain. Even as Peter unhooked his mask, the critical link slid squealing over the flange of the porthole. There was a violent rattling, a frightened shout, a wild capsizing tilt and the capsule slid out of its chains. Slowly at first, then with gathering momentum they spun down and round into the darkening sea.

The dials of the instruments rotated in front of Peter's eyes, the depth guage rushing towards him, now magnified to a nightmare obesity, now receding to a distant pinpoint; and mixed up with the instruments were the faces of Wendy, Richard and Anne. Poor kids, he thought: first their mother and now their father. God, what a mess he had made of things. He searched for something to hang on to in his last few seconds of life, and Jean came walking towards him, smiling, out of the walls of the capsule. He reached for her; but as his arms were about to go round her, she faded wraithlike into the dials of the instrument panel, and there in her place stood the girl from the trawler smiling at him tongue between teeth. It bewildered and distressed him that in his moment of dying he should be thinking not of his wife but of a girl he had met only once: and she, as likely as not, a slut from the Italian underworld.

The grate of the hacksaw rose to a crescendo, drowning the rasp of his breath and filling the capsule with waves of discordant sound. Then, suddenly, as if from the edge of another world, he heard the snap of parting metal. He felt the capsule hang for a moment completely motionless and then start rising, fast and straight, for the surface. He remembered thinking (as though all this were happening not to him but to somebody else) that the ballast weights must have been sawed away; he remembered thinking too that salvation had come just a handful of seconds too late. Then the voice of the doctor was booming over the loud-hailer: "Hang on! Hang on for just another minute and we'll have you out." But with his head aspin and the waves of carbon-dioxide poisoning sweeping through him with every breath, hanging on was easier said than done.

Hang on! Hang on! Hang on! Scott-Henderson's voice reechoed from wall to wall like a boomerang. It wasn't in Peter's nature to throw up the sponge. He screwed up his eyes and clamped his hands tight round the sample bar of gold, while foam came dribbling out of his mouth, his lips turned blue and a terrible ache spread burning through the walls of his lungs. He lost consciousness as the capsule came bursting out of the water only a few yards from *Oyster*'s stern.

But he had hung on long enough. And when Scott-Henderson, gagging and choking in the poisoned air, dragged him from capsule to decompression chamber, he was still alive.

Within half an hour of surfacing, with breathing masks clamped firmly to their mouths and an injection of Largactil in their veins, both Peter and the senior diver were out of danger. Within an hour they were sleeping the sleep of the deeply drugged, while *Oyster* turned her wake to the dawn and stood west into the Gulf of Sidra.

CHAPTER 10

It was thirty hours before he woke; soon after he had been carried from decompression chamber to cabin. The sun was streaming over his bunk, and for several minutes he lay motionless, luxuriating in its warmth and the thankfulness of being alive. He felt weak but by no means ill, with only the slightest hint of a headache and nothing to show for his ordeal except a bruise on the back of his head and a hypodermic mark on his arm. After a while he climbed cautiously out of bed and peered through the porthole.

Oyster was riding at anchor in the center of a shallow bay that he didn't recognize. The bay was void of shipping, but a line of marker buoys sparkling in the sun indicated that it was not always so deserted. It was the pipeline and storage tanks that eventually gave him the clue. They must, he surmised, be at Marsa Brega: the terminal of the desert oil lines, about a hundred and fifty miles to the south of Benghazi.

"Back to your bunk!" Scott-Henderson was eyeing him with disapproval from the doorway.

"What's been happening? How's Al?"

"Into the bunk, if you want to know." While he took

Peter's temperature and blood pressure the doctor brought him up to date with the news.

As he learned of the homing aid, Joe Blair's death and the frogmen's efforts at boarding, Peter's eyes grew wider and wider, and when Scott-Henderson came to describe how Ken had been knifed he swung out of bed. "I want to see him. Please."

Scott-Henderson laughed. "He was only nicked. The shock didn't do his head any good, but you two are a hard pair to keep down, and he was up and about again this morning. The truth is we've all been damned lucky."

"All except Joe Blair."

"Yes. Next time—if there *is* a next time—we'll very likely end up the way he did."

Peter's voice was thoughtful. "So you reckon we ought to leave the gold where it is?"

"That's not for me to decide. But I gather Gary's holding a meeting this evening. Now I want you to stay in bed for lunch."

It was not in fact until *Oyster* was squared off for the night that the four of them—Malloy, McArthur, Ken and Peter—settled down to talk things over in the saloon.

It was a Very Serious Meeting. Gone now was the happy-go-lucky atmosphere of a search for pirate gold; for they had learned the hard way, with men's lives, that the Rommel treasure wasn't going to drop into their hands without a fight.

Malloy didn't waste time with small talk. "Now we're back on our feet we must decide what happens next. The question is, do we carry on with salvage or do we call the whole operation off? Mr. McArthur, I'd appreciate your views."

"I'm a Scot, sir, and I hate to think of all that gold goin' to waste on the bed of the sea. On the other hand I value my life more than gold."

"So what's your decision?"

"It's a mighty hard decision to have to make. If I may I'd

like to sleep on it." McArthur, it was clear, had decided to sit on the fence.

"Ken, how do *you* feel?"

There was no doubt to which side of the fence Ken Richards wanted to descend. He wanted to call the search off, at least for the time being, to return to Europe and organize another and larger expedition with adequate security. Peter was surprised, until his observer's motives were brought to light. Ken Richards was all too aware that it was his information which had triggered off the search, and now that the search was costing other men their lives he felt both responsible and guilty. A more ruthless character would have consoled himself with the thought that one can't make an omelette without breaking eggs. But Ken, when the going got tough, was too tender-hearted to want to see things through.

Malloy had no such scruples. "I can't follow you there, Kenneth. The crew are getting a bonus; I told them there'd be danger, and if they're not happy they can sign off. In my opinion, now we know where the gold is, we'd be crazy not to go flat out to raise it. But what's your view, Peter?"

Malloy would have laid a pound to a penny on the reply; for he recognized that behind the façade of a staid solicitor lay a core of toughness and obstinacy that the years had done nothing to corrode. And Peter didn't disappoint him. "I'm damned," he said slowly, "if I'll be scared off by a bunch of thugs. I vote for carrying on—but with certain safeguards, to be very sure there's no repetition of what went on the night before last."

Malloy nodded. "The safeguards go without saying. We're not kids playing at buccaneer. But what sort of thing had you in mind?"

Everyone had different ideas. For a while Malloy let the conversation ebb to and fro, then quietly and succinctly he summed up the essence of what was wanted. "As I see it, there are four requisites of success.

"First, we need a new base. I'm sure we none of us want to go back to Benghazi, to be spied on by sponge boats and fishing boats and God knows how many other boats. Now as long as we don't involve our hosts in trouble Marsa Brega would be ideal—cut off from the rest of Libya and guarded by the oil companies' patrols—and I've got permission for us to stay as long as we want to.

"Second, we need to make a thorough overhaul of *Oyster* and *Pearl*. God knows what damage the explosions may have done. We'll certainly have to fly in replacement equipment. We *may* have to go into dry dock, and if this is the case then we'll definitely have to call the search off for the time being. But may I suggest you leave this to me? I assure you I wouldn't even think of salvage until literally every nut and bolt in *Oyster* and *Pearl* has been tested and proved.

"Third, we need security. And by security I mean some method of keeping guard while the treasure is being raised, and *some* method of getting it away the moment it's off the bed of the sea—the one thing we want to avoid is having to make the voyage to Malta with our decks piled high with gold. Now I've a suggestion here . . . It was your idea in the first place, Peter, at our meeting in the Dorchester. An amphibian. At a guess I'd vote for a Grumman Albatross or a Bolus Sea Horse. A plane that could circle overhead and keep watch while we're diving, *and* could land on the water and pick up the gold the moment it's raised and fly it direct to Geneva."

The idea of using an amphibian was, they had to admit, attractive. "And the last requisite?" Ken's voice was thoughtful.

"Cooperation from the Libyan Police. I suggest we ask them for protection. We needn't go too deeply into the whys and wherefores; we could just say we were attacked by the Mafia and that while we're in Libyan waters we'd appreciate their help."

They talked through two pots of coffee and half a dozen of Malloy's cigars. They talked till the belt of Orion swung high into the midnight sky, and a dry south wind came moaning in from the desert, swirling little streamers of sand across the anchorage. Peter was tired, and as time passed he settled back in his chair and let the conversation flow over and round him. He would have liked to close his eyes, but whenever he shut them for more than a few minutes he was haunted by a vision that he couldn't get out of his mind—the vision of Gina's suntanned body drifting broken among the frogmen's: as if, he thought angrily, it mattered what had happened to her. For hadn't it been made abundantly clear that she was mixed up with the Mafia? He suddenly heard Malloy's voice, as if from a long way away. "If we can't get a second pilot perhaps Peter could fly her?"

He became very much awake. "What's that!"

"I was saying that we really need two divers for *Pearl* and two pilots for the amphibian. The divers I'm pretty sure I can get, but I only know one pilot I'd want to bring in on a thing like this. Could you fly an Albatross or a Sea Horse?"

He shook his head. "I did about a hundred hours on Walrus amphibians in the war. But I haven't flown since the R.N.V.R. squadrons packed in—must be all of ten years ago."

"But in an emergency?"

He yawned. "I *might* get you down in one piece. But I certainly wouldn't count on it!"

The conversation dragged on for another hour. It was past midnight before their plans were finalized and they at last dossed down to the slap of a rising sea and the roar of wind from the desert.

Next morning the *ghibli* was again in full spate and Marsa was grey with wind-blown sand. Malloy went ashore early and spent the better part of the day on the oil company's telephone—and hearing how smoothly he dealt with their requirements Peter could well understand how he had come to be head of one of the largest oil combines in Texas. By the evening he had everything fixed—patrols by the oil companies' security guards, a Bolus Sea Horse and spares being flown in from Nice, and an interview in Benghazi the following afternoon with the Cyrenaican Chief of Police.

Because they had agreed never to travel alone Malloy had booked two seats on the plane from Marsa to Benghazi, and Peter asked if he could keep him company. Since Ken was not fit enough to fly and the rest of the crew would be needed for repair work, this seemed the obvious arrangement.

They took off the following afternoon.

The flight to Benghazi was dusty and bumpy and none too comfortable, but at least with the wind behind them they made good time. They were met at the airport by a police Mercedes, and within half an hour of touchdown were being escorted through the maze of palm-lined courtyards which led to the offices of Colonel Omar Rafik, head of the Cyrenaican Police.

The interview that followed was something of an eye-opener.

The colonel, a spare ascetic Muslim of indeterminate age, greeted them with a mixture of oriental courtesy and western briskness. "Welcome, gentlemen, to Benghazi. Please be seated and tell me how I can help you."

It was Malloy who did the talking. "We've a rather unusual request, Colonel. We've come to ask for police protection."

"Protection against whom?"

"The Mafia."

"And how, may I ask, have such respectable gentlemen as yourselves become involved with the Mafia?"

Malloy had his story all worked out. As a retired oil man he was, he said, interested in the possibility of discovering natural gas under the Gulf of Sidra. He had been taking samples from the bed of the sea when his yacht was boarded and ransacked by the Mafia. "We were lucky," he added with a great show of indignation, "to get away with our lives."

When he had finished there was a brief silence, then the colonel said quietly. "Mr. Malloy, since you are unwilling to put your cards on the table I regret I cannot help you."

"But you surely want to protect us: as visitors to your country?"

The colonel's pencil drummed softly on the inlaid marble of his desk. "I appreciate that in *your* country we in the eastern Mediterranean are thought of as devious and deceitful, and it is doubtless because of this that you feel justified in trying to pull the cotton wool over my eyes."

"What cotton wool?"

"Mr. Malloy! It is common gossip in the bazaars that you are here to search for the Rommel treasure."

He was very much taken aback; he had been to considerable pains to keep the *raison d'être* of *Oyster*'s visit a secret. He looked at Colonel Rafik with a new respect. "In that case, sir, I apologize and rephrase my request: will you afford us your protection while we try to raise it?"

A shrug and a turning up of palms. "Much to my regret the Rommel treasure is outside Libyan waters at the moment."

"At the moment?"

The colonel's eyes turned briefly to Peter. "Your friend is a lawyer. He doubtless knows what countries have petitioned the United Nations for an extension of territorial waters."

"Libya hasn't"—this was a point that Peter had been careful to check—"not at the end of last month."

"The petition, Mr. Grey, was lodged only a few days ago. I understand that our delegate will soon be chairman of the appropriate committee."

Malloy and Peter looked at one another. Here was a spur

if ever they needed one to keep things moving. Malloy got to his feet. He could see how it was. Colonel Rafik was being completely open with them; he had gone out of his way to be helpful, and it would be expecting altogether too much that he should assist them in raising the treasure now when in a couple of months it might well lie within Libyan jurisdiction. He held out his hand. "Thank you for your hospitality, Colonel. And our apologies for wasting your time."

Again Rafik's eyes met Peter's. "One of my men will do what he can to help you, but unofficially." He turned to Malloy. "Like your friend Mr. Grey I fought with the Eighth Army, and I am no friend of the Mafia's."

They were ushered politely out through the palm-green courts.

On the way to the Berenice Hotel Malloy was unusually quiet. Not till they were sipping coffee on the terrace did he give an indication of what he was thinking. "It's a long time," he said slowly, "since I've felt so thoroughly put in my place."

Peter nodded; he felt a bit the same way; but his mind was on other things—for they happened by coincidence to have sat at the table at which he and Gina—was it really only five days ago?—had sipped their Mineralé and bitter lemon. He refused a second cup of coffee and stared absentmindedly at the darkening waters of the harbour. After a while he pushed back his chair: "Excuse me a minute, Gary. I'll not be long."

He walked down the terrace, through the foyer and up to the reception desk to where a pale-faced clerk was reading a magazine from the Foreign Languages Press, Peking. He cleared his throat.

The clerk marked his place with a length of rice paper and looked up.

"The young Italian lady in room forty-two: is she still staying in the hotel?"

The clerk took a careful look at him, then pulled out his ledger. "Signorina Tacchini? Yes, she is booked for one more week. You wish to speak with her?"

"No. But I wonder if you'd mind telling me: was she in the hotel for breakfast this morning?"

An even more careful look; then, with a shrug, the clerk ran his pencil down the ledger. "Yes, she had breakfast in her room."

"Thank you."

It was quite ridiculous, he told himself, that he should feel thankful. The girl was one of the Mafia; she had fobbed him off with a pack of lies; she had planted the homing aid that had cost upward of a dozen men their lives; and here he was asking tenderly after her health like a moonstruck lover . . . Gina Tacchini. The name was vaguely familiar; but in what connection he couldn't for the life of him think. He puzzled over it on the return flight to Marsa Brega; but the link that would have explained so much escaped him.

The next week was unexciting though not uneventful.

The Sea Horse arrived the following afternoon: a solid-looking amphibian with a payload of several tons. It brought in a mass of replacement equipment (new chains, a hook for the nosecap, weights, air hoses and waterproof electric cables), also a couple of divers to take the place of Joe Blair; but there was only one pilot, Bob Blasingame an ex-bush operator who was a personal friend of Malloy.

At Malloy's suggestion as soon as Blasingame had settled in he took Peter for a series of practice flights, with the idea of having two pilots who could handle the Sea Horse in an emergency. So all that week, while the crew set to work refurbishing *Oyster* and *Pearl,* Peter did circuits and bumps.

He was keyed up and nervous at first. It was the better part of a decade since he had done any flying, and the Bolus was a good deal heavier than anything he had handled in the Air Arm. On the first day he did little more than familiarize himself with the controls; on the second day he took over for only a few minutes; but on the third day his confidence quite suddenly came back, and by the end of a week he was flying the Sea Horse solo. Landing was what he had always been good at, and after a series of near-perfect touchdowns Blasingame paid him the compliment of saying he would fly with him anywhere.

Oyster and her equipment, meanwhile, were being given a thorough overhaul.

She had been lucky. The grenade had buckled a number of plates in her hull but her screws and her underwater viewing chamber had escaped injury; her capsule too had suffered no more than superficial damage; and round about the time that Peter was making his first landings, *Oyster* put to sea for her deep-water tests. The *ghibli* by this time had subsided, conditions for diving were near-perfect, and Malloy was able to make descents to one hundred, two hundred, and finally to three hundred feet. And everything worked so smoothly that even the perfectionist McArthur was satisfied that their equipment was back at a hundred per cent efficiency.

They had hoped, all the time they had been sheltering in the oil companies' base at Marsa Brega, that their whereabouts was unknown to the Mafia; but the day after completing their tests they suffered a rude awakening.

Peter had been lending a hand during the afternoon with servicing the Sea Horse; but round about four o'clock his interest in the plane was superseded by his interest in the tea that he knew would be brewing in *Oyster*'s galley, so he set off to walk the odd quarter of a mile from airstrip to quay.

His route took him over the track that ran between the Tripoli/Benghazi road and the harbour. As he crossed the tarmac he noticed, half hidden by the sand dunes, a car, and beside the car a figure watching the airstrip through binoculars. The figure was familiar: and, in blue denim slacks and a golden headsquare, very nice too.

He was almost up to her before a stone slipped under his foot and rolled with a clatter into the ditch at the side of the road. She turned with a start, and her eyes lit up. "Peter! Thank God you're still alive!"

His pleasure at seeing her was quickly metamorphosed to anger as he reminded himself of what she was and what she had done. "No thanks to you."

His anger got through to her, and she moved warily to the opposite side of the Alfa Romeo. They stared at each other over the windshield.

"You're very handy," he said, "at sticking homing aids on to other people's boats."

She curtsied. "Thank you kindly, sir, she said."

"Doesn't it worry you that that little escapade cost a lot of your friends their lives?"

She was more amused than angry. "You're like a little boy with a sum that he can't understand. You put two and two together and think you're clever when you make the answer five!"

He came to a sudden decision. He was fed up with verbal sparring; why shouldn't he grab her and carry her off to *Oyster* and find out once and for all what she was playing at? He began to edge round the Alfa Romeo. "I think," he said with a smile, "that it's time you and I had another dinner together."

She jumped back. She pulled out a Beretta and levelled it, disconcertingly straight, at his stomach. "I'm so sorry, Mr. Grey. I've a prior engagement for dinner."

He cursed himself for a fool; he might have guessed she'd be armed. "You didn't play so hard to get last time."

She motioned him back with her gun. "Last time I felt sure your intentions were honourable."

"They are now."

The gun didn't waver as she slid gracefully into the driving seat. James Bond, he felt sure, would have jumped her as she fumbled with the ignition key; but he was a great deal too fond of life to risk it.

"Who," she said, "are you trying to fool? Kidnap and a spot of torture and rape is what you were thinking of!"

The engine roared. And the Alfa Romeo slid into gear and disappeared in the direction of Benghazi in a swirl of dust.

He felt a complete fool. Angry, frustrated and dismayed: angry at being outsmarted by a slip of a girl, frustrated because she still remained an enigma—in spite of all the evidence he still couldn't bring himself to believe that she was nothing more than a Sicilian tart, and dismayed because he realized that her presence at the airstrip could mean only one thing—they had been tracked down and were being watched by the Mafia. He hurried to the quay, where *Oyster* was swinging quietly against her moorings.

When Malloy heard what had happened he pulled a long face, and called Peter, Ken, McArthur and Blasingame to his cabin.

It was a problem to know what to do. Their first reaction was to call things off for the time being: to return to Europe and get together another and larger expedition, this time with official protection, say in the shape of a naval gunboat. But this would take time. And time was no longer their ally; for they knew now that the treasure might soon be transferred, from international waters to Libyan.

"Could we wait for another *ghibli*"—this was Ken's suggestion—"you know how dark it gets; we might be able to slip away and have the treasure up before they realized we'd gone?"

The idea didn't please Blasingame. "We couldn't use the Sea Horse in a *ghibli*."

"And we can't," Malloy added, "hang on indefinitely at

Marsa. We're the companies' guests, and now we know we're being spied on we can't involve them in danger."

It was Peter who voiced what they were all subconsciously thinking. "The plane's ready. *Oyster*'s finished her trials. We'll never have a better chance to raise it than now."

They didn't make up their minds without a great deal of heart-searching. And when they *had* made them up, they laid their plans with the most painstaking care. For they appreciated now that it was more than six million pounds that was at stake. It was their lives.

CHAPTER 11

THEY slipped out of Marsa Brega as soon as it was dark.

Most of the crew, aware of the full day's program ahead, turned in early; but Ken and the master stayed on deck, sharing the bridge and the slow unfolding beauty of the night. And it was a night to remember. For as they stood north into the Gulf of Sidra the cloud dispersed to frame a scattering of gemlike stars and the oriflamme of a rising moon. By midnight the sea was gold as a *louis d'or*. There was no sound except the continuous hiss of their bow wave (for they were travelling fast), and no movement except the rhythmic sway of their masts against a backdrop of sky.

But the beauty of the night meant little to Ken as he went over and over their plans, searching anxiously for the flaw that could cost them their lives. By the time he turned in they were nearing the approaches to Benghazi.

They hove to in the search area in the pale half-light of dawn.

Away in the east the Libyan plateau rose indistinctly out of a haze pierced at regular intervals by the group flashing four of the Sidi Sueicher beacon, the only sign of life in a world of aquamarine and mother of pearl. Everything was hushed and still as they dropped anchor above the treasure. The capsule was swung over the side; cameras, arcs and suction pump were lowered to the bed of the sea; then they waited, keyed up, for the Sea Horse.

They had everything worked out.

The key was speed.

Peter and Malloy would make a quick reconnaissance to locate and take samples from the crates, then the divers would work flat-out, two at a time, to raise what treasure they could before they were disturbed . . . They lifted their binoculars, impatiently, to the sky in the south.

She came dead on time, at a few minutes to six a.m.: first the offbeat throb of her engines then the glint of gold on her wings. Blasingame circled them at three thousand feet, took a careful look round and flashed them the prearranged all clear.

"Right?" A nod from Peter, and Malloy snapped shut the air locks. "Lower away."

And to the rattle of chains and the hiss of oxy-helium they were let down to the bed of the sea.

It was very different from last time; for the water, bright in the light of the sun, was now alive with colour: every shade of blue from aquamarine to indigo, and for contrast little shoals of red and orange fish (sea bream, gurnard and yellowtail) which nibbled playfully at the air bubbles as they went streaming past the porthole. But as they descended the sea lost its luminosity until by the time they reached three hundred feet they were in semidarkness.

The capsule jerked to a stop. They waited. And suddenly, at an order from the salvage vessel, a whole battery of arc lamps, suspended some twenty feet over their heads, was switched on, throwing the bed of the sea into vivid relief. They checked the pressure. They opened the hatches. And swam into fairyland.

It was like the most fabulous of Aladdin's caves. In the center was the capsule, its metal aglow like phosphorous in the refracted light of the arcs, and beside it the staring eyes of the cameras and the snakelike coil of the suction tubes. While scattered about on the sand were all the stage props of treasure trove: the hacksaw that the diver had dropped as he cut off their ballast weights, the skeleton of the *Selina*'s lifeboat, the half-dismantled crate with its bars of gold spilt out on the sand, and a random pattern of little mounds rising like fairy rings from the bed of the sea. It was the last of these that claimed their attention.

The first of the mounds that they examined turned out to be screening, much to their chagrin, nothing more exciting than an outcrop of rock, the home of a small and very frightened octopus. But under the second and third they discovered crates.

They used the suction pump to siphon them clear of sand. They used a hacksaw to cut through the rust-green hinges. A wrench, and the lids went spinning weightlessly away; and there in crumbling hessian bags lay mound after mound of inch to inch-and-a-half discs, heavy and deeply engraved. They picked them up and ran them through their fingers: skein after skein of sovereigns, *louis d'or* and Maria Theresa crowns. They had expected the treasure to be there; and yet now it was literally trickling through their fingers they could hardly believe it. They moved as if in a dream from crate to crate.

They discovered six, all within a radius of twenty to thirty yards. Two contained gold and black-coated silver bars; two contained coins (mostly *louis d'or*); one contained boxes of paper currency (some of it badly discoloured), and one contained jewels and *objets d'art.*

While Malloy made a sketch of the crates' positions and contents, Peter loaded samples into a series of polythene bags. They then swam quickly back to the capsule: quickly, because Malloy was anxious to direct operations from *Oyster*'s deck, and the longer that he and Peter spent on the seabed the longer they would have to spend subsequently in the decompression chamber. They sealed themselves in and were winched posthaste to the surface.

By seven a.m. they were resting comfortably in the chamber, their decompression under way, while the samples they had brought up were tested for purity and the second pair of divers were being sealed into *Pearl*. Between mouthfuls of toast and sips of coffee they talked over the intercom to the doctor.

"Is the capsule back on the bottom?" Malloy was fretful of even the slightest delay.

"It's on the way down."

"And the Bolus is overhead?"

"Everything's fine. Relax."

"That's easier said than done. How much longer before we're out?"

"About an hour."

"Jesus wept! Can't you speed things up?"

"You can come out right away if you don't mind being crippled for life with the bends."

Time passed slowly, but it wasn't wasted. For as the helium content of the air in the decompression chamber was progressively reduced, the crew got ready the impedimenta of salvage. Wooden boxes for packing away the treasure were brought on deck, cranes were swung over the side, grab nets were lowered to the bed of the sea, and in the saloon the samples that Peter and Malloy had brought up were tested with aqua regia.

And the tests were positive. The bars when cleaned and sawn in half turned out to be twenty-carat gold, while the coins when given the acid test dissolved according to the book. The jewels it was not so easy to be sure of, and it seemed to Ken that some of them were a bit too big to be genuine. They therefore decided to raise the bars and the sovereigns first, then the jewels and the paper currency, if they had time, last.

Eight o'clock, and sand siphoning up through the pumps and whirling away like a miniature *ghibli* over the surface of the sea, the grab nets maneuvering into position, and the divers transferring the bags of coin from seabed to nets. They could watch it all on the screen of the television: the darting fish, the air bubbles slanting out of the hookah-type tubes, and the great mounds of coin (near-weightless at three hundred feet) being transferred gradually into the nets. A signal from the senior diver, a rattle and hum from the winch, and just as Peter and Malloy were emerging from the decompression chamber the first consignment of the Rommel treasure came swinging over the side.

It didn't look all that impressive; rather like so many bars of lead and discs of ebony; only here and there where the coins were cut or rubbed clean did they catch sight of the provocative glitter of gold.

It was their moment of triumph: the vindication of all that the three of them had worked for and dreamed of.

It seemed almost too easy to be true, as, watched by the circling Sea Horse, they unloaded the nets and stacked the coin (thousands of pounds worth at a time) into the waiting boxes. The coins were elusive; several of the bags burst as they hit the deck, showering the scuppers with sovereigns, crowns and *louis d'or*, and the second consignment was on its way up before they had cleared the deck of the first. It was a nice thought: that their wealth was now limited only by the time they were taking to pack it into the waiting boxes!

As the sun climbed high into a cloudless sky the divers moved on to the second of the *Selina*'s cases. It was bars now instead of coins, and the bars were not so easy to handle: heavier and more liable to tip out of the nets. The case was no more than half salvaged when they picked up the message they had been dreading. "Sea Horse to *Oyster*. Two sponge divers approaching from Tocra. Range fifteen miles."

They were taking no chances. "Prepare for emergency recall." Malloy's voice was sharp. "If they close to three miles, raise the capsule and run."

The divers were alerted; the lookouts were doubled; McArthur, binoculars round his neck, swarmed into the crow's nest; and the circling amphibian reported the spongers' progress. "They're heading straight towards you: range twelve-to-thirteen miles . . . They don't seem to be in any great hurry: making about four to five knots . . . Not many crew on deck, no divers, and as far as I can see no special equipment like rockets or guns . . ."

They were on tenterhooks as the boats crept gradually nearer: ten miles, eight miles, six miles. Malloy was about to haul in the capsule and run, when to everyone's surprise the sponge divers dropped anchor. They could hear the disbelief in Blasingame's voice. "They're losing way; they've hove to; they've let out their anchors." A pause; then, incredulously: "They're lowering seine nets! They can't really think we'll believe they're going to fish!"

From *Oyster*'s deck they could just make out the squat silhouettes drifting idly against a backdrop of dunes. Malloy picked up the portable radio. "Go down and see what they're up to."

Four times the Sea Horse flew low over the drifting spongers. "They look quite normal," Blasingame's voice was puzzled. "No guns, no underwater equipment, no divers. And they're actually catching fish!"

"Keep watching. Go in low every now and then, when they're not expecting it. And call us if you see anything odd."

They didn't like it. But they didn't see how the spongers, from a range of four to five miles, could harm them. So they put out a dinghy and an extra pair of divers (armed with Biochiarellis) to patrol between them and the sponge boats, and carried on with salvaging the treasure.

And the hours passed, and the bars of gold and the *louis d'or* came streaming up from the bed of the sea, and the wooden boxes were filled and stacked tier upon tier in *Oyster*'s stern until by midmorning the working space aft was piled high with gold to the value of well over a million pounds.

And all the while the sponge boats lay idle in the sun, quite happy, apparently, to watch.

At eleven-thirty they changed divers. The first pair had been on the bed of the sea for more than four hours; cold, exhausted and with their bloodstream saturated with oxy-helium, they were now hauled up and left to rest in the comfort and warmth of the decompression chamber. Here they would have to remain for over twenty-four hours. But their work went on, with their successors going down in the capsule and opening up the fourth of the *Selina*'s cases.

They had a temporary disappointment here; for the case turned out to be in two compartments, one holding gold and one silver. They hadn't the carrying capacity to bother with metal worth a mere ten shillings an ounce; so they turned their attention to the case holding diamonds and *objets d'art.* Church plate and delicate works in filigree hardly look their best when tarnished by twenty-five years under the sea; but even so as the chalices, crowns and necklaces were hauled on deck and roughly cleaned, Malloy realized that they might well have something here that would be worth even more than the *louis d'or.*

By half past one the case was empty. And still the spongers made not the slightest move. There was something unnerving about their passivity.

They knew that some time during the afternoon the amphibian would run short of fuel, and that this would be the moment of danger—when Blasingame was obliged to return to Marsa to top up his tanks, leaving them for roughly an hour and a half devoid of air cover. But they had made their plans carefully. Before the Sea Horse left them they intended to up-anchor and use their superior speed to shake the sponge boats off; they would then make for a prearranged rendezvous, following a track that would take them close to the passenger liner *Citta di Livorno* which was homeward bound that evening from Benghazi to Naples. (Even the Mafia, Malloy felt, were hardly likely to try and hijack them within full view of a passenger liner!) They checked the details of timing and rendezvous.

"*Oyster* to Sea Horse. When do you want to leave?"

"Hello, *Oyster*. Not for a couple of hours. I suggest fifteen-thirty."

"Roger. And how long will you be away for?"

"Estimate an hour and a half."

"Roger again. Check the rendezvous."

"D.Q.P.S. east: L.E.X.K. north."

Malloy checked the code. "Rendezvous agreed. We'll meet you there at seventeen hundred. Stay circling in the meanwhile."

They had hoped that the men on the bed of the sea would be able to continue working until it was time for *Oyster* to get under way. But soon after two o'clock both divers began to complain of cold—one of the disadvantages of oxy-helium is that it sucks the warmth out of the tissues. Malloy therefore decided that for the last hour of salvaging he would go down himself, accompanied by the standby diver. It was not an ideal arrangement; but with so many of the crew tied up with the mechanics of decompression it was the best they could think of—and it had at least the advantage that Malloy could see for himself the extent of the treasure that was having to be left behind. By fourteen-thirty hours he and Mearns were on the bed of the sea, and the other divers, having climbed through the air lock, were sipping coffee in the warmth of the decompression chamber.

And still the sponge boats swung idle against their anchors, watching.

At a few minutes to fifteen-thirty hours *Oyster* prepared to get under way. The safety patrol was brought in, equipment was winched to within a couple of feet of the surface, and Malloy and Mearns climbed back into *Pearl* for the ascent. By now three-quarters of the treasure had been salvaged. It went against the grain to leave behind them nearly a couple of million pounds worth of silver, paper currency and gold; but they had so much already in their hands that it was not worth taking a risk for the sake of a few bars more.

A signal from McArthur and they hauled in capsule, arc lamps and cameras. Fast. Dinghy and divers were hoist over the rail. The anchor came whirling aboard. And with a roar of engines, *Oyster* leapt seaward in a flurry of spray.

They expected the sponge boats to try and follow.

But they didn't. They remained at anchor, fishing, not bothering even to haul in their nets. And this once again was unnerving; for it suggested that the Mafia, too, had a plan.

They headed west, flat out, bow waves creaming the length of their hull. Within five minutes the sponge boats had disappeared from sight; within fifteen they had disappeared from the radar screen, and *Oyster*, except for the circling Sea Horse, was alone.

Blasingame took a careful look round. From three thousand feet he had a magnificent view: east to the golden sweep of the Cyrenaican shore, west to the empty reaches of the Mediterranean, and north to the cumulus piled high over the distant mountains of Crete. There were only two ships in sight: immediately beneath him *Oyster*, and away in the southwest the tiny silhouette of the *Citta di Livorno* nosing out of Benghazi harbour. There was no hint of anything unusual, no sign of the Mafia, and not the slightest suspicion of danger. He waggled his wings, opened his throttles and set course for Marsa Brega.

On *Oyster*'s deck, as they watched the Sea Horse recede to a pinpoint, they told themselves that they had nothing to worry about. And yet, against all the dictates of reason, as she vanished over the horizon they felt naked, vulnerable and afraid.

Peter kept watch to starboard. He was nervous. He couldn't think why, for with the sky empty and their radar screen as blank as a glassless window, there wasn't the slightest hint of danger. He kept on telling himself that their plans were foolproof, that the Mafia couldn't possibly know where they were and that even if they did there wasn't a thing they could do about it. Yet he still had the feeling that something was wrong. He kept peering through his binoculars at sea and sky, as though he half-expected the Mafia to surface by submarine or come parachuting out of the sun. He told himself that that sort of thing didn't happen: not in real life. But his fears refused to subside; they were simply, as time went by, pushed into the background.

By half past four they were nearing the rendezvous, and still the sea and the sky were innocent as the eyes of a nun. They cruised up and down, waiting, watching the sun sink slowly seaward and the clouds pile up over the distant island of Crete. Everything was very quiet; the beat of their engines reduced to a soundless vibration, and half the ship's company immured in the decompression chamber.

Peter, for want of something better to do, made a check on the wooden boxes. There were over sixty of them, with the gold well hidden and, as an added precaution, labelled *"Specimens: Institute of Marine Biology, Geneva."* Within a couple of hours, if all went well, the boxes would be loaded into the Sea Horse; by midnight they would be in Geneva;

by early next morning they would be safe in the vaults of the Banque Helvétia. If all went well . . .

As the hands of their watches crept snail-like to five o'clock they peered hopefully at the sky in the south. But there was no sign of the approaching amphibian.

They were not, at first, all that worried: a head wind, a couple of degrees of error in Blasingame's course, a tea break for the ground crew—there were any number of things that could be causing a few minutes' delay. But as time passed and the sky remained inviolate, McArthur began to pace the bridge. He was about to give Blasingame a call when they spotted a pinhead of black on the horizon; and within half a minute they had identified—much to their relief—the silhouette of the Sea Horse.

Blasingame was coming in fast. Realizing he was late, he didn't bother with a preliminary circuit, but turned straight into wind to land. And what a landing he made! He must, Peter thought, be as keyed up as the rest of them; for he hit the water awkwardly, dipping in his starboard float and raising a great fountain of spray. Then he taxied towards them, getting into position to pick up the tow rope which *Oyster* was trailing astern.

It isn't easy for a pilot to maneuver a twin-engined amphibian on to a rope and pick it up by himself; so Peter and Ken (as had been agreed) put out in the dinghy to help. As they neared the Sea Horse they could see Blasingame quite clearly, hunched up over the controls. As they came alongside he shouted something and turned down his thumb. They couldn't hear what he said because of the roar of the engines, but Peter assumed that he was registering disgust at his landing. They picked up the tow rope, attached it to the nose of the Sea Horse and rowed aft to the hatch in the side of the fuselage.

They had no hint of fear as they waited for Blasingame to open the hatch, and no premonition of disaster. But as the door creaked open they heard a sudden thud and a grunt of pain. They looked at each other. They grabbed the hatch and peered in, and saw Blasingame face down on the deck plates in a pool of blood. For a second they froze, numb with shock. Then, as their eyes grew accustomed to the dark interior of the plane, they saw something else: a man, crouched in the shadows, his gun lining up on them.

As the Sea Horse with no one at the controls swung uneasily in the cross swell, a shaft of light flicked briefly over the gunman's face. It was a face that Peter hadn't seen for twenty-five years. But he recognized it at once. Cruel eyes, slit mouth, and the lantern jaw of a fanatic: the face of Lieutenant Schultz.

CHAPTER 12

THERE was a sort of poetic justice to it: that the three of them who twenty-five years ago had seen the gold go down, should at the moment of its salvage be again brought face to face in a final *dénouement.*

"So we meet again." The clipped voice hadn't changed with the years. "Come aboard. One at a time. And slowly." His gun was steady, and they knew that he wouldn't hesitate to use it.

"Have you killed him?" Ken dropped to his knees by the crumpled figure of the pilot.

"*He* will live. *You,* if you aren't careful, won't be so lucky."

Ken cradled Blasingame's head in his lap, using his handkerchief to staunch the blood that was oozing out of a gash in the back of the pilot's neck. He was white with anger. "You bastard. You won't get away with this."

The German smiled. His finger tightened on the trigger, and a bullet whipped the handkerchief out of Ken's hand. "Order your crew to bring the gold to the plane. At once. And quickly. Or"—the Walther lined up on Peter—"I shall shoot your friend in the stomach."

Peter could feel the sweat break out on his forehead. He thought of making a dive for the gun; but as his eyes met Schultz's, he knew that he wouldn't stand a chance.

Ken Richards didn't appear to take the threat very seriously; he seemed more interested in watching the door of an inspection panel, a couple of yards behind the German's back. "If we brought the plane alongside," he said mildly, "she'd be easier to load."

Schultz shook his head. "The order. Now. Or your friend has exactly ten seconds to live."

The seconds ticked by. The sweat ran cold into Peter's eyes.

There was a grate of metal, and the inspection panel swung open.

Her denim slacks were black with oil, and her golden head-square was tied as a bandage over her arm, but her voice and her Beretta were steady. "Drop your gun, Schultz."

They saw the German's face first stiffen with fear, then twist into a snarl of pathological rage. They could appreciate how he felt; they could almost sympathize—after years of plotting and planning to have the gold so nearly within his grasp and then to be thwarted literally at the last second by a girl with a toy Beretta!

"Don't try anything silly." Ken's voice was sharp, a warning as much to Gina as to the German; he edged sideways to widen the angle of fire.

"I shall count three," the girl sounded very sure of herself. "And if you don't drop your gun. I shall shoot you in the back of the leg . . . One, two—"

Schultz leaned forward as if to lay his gun on the deck plates; but at the last second he swallow-dived to the left, snapping a shot over his shoulder as he fell. It was a good shot but it wasn't quite good enough, the bullet smacking into the bulkhead an inch from Gina's head. Her revolver cracked once, and the German doubled up, his Walther clattering to the deck. There was a second of absolute silence; then with a half-snarl half-cough Schultz made a grab for his gun. She fired again. Then again and again and again, the bullets jerking the German this way and that like a string-pulled marionette as he struggled to line up his gun. Not until the Beretta was empty did he at last lie mercifully still.

A shocked silence and the Sea Horse with no one at the controls teetering uneasily, and Peter going up to the girl and taking the gun very gently out of her hand. She was trembling, dead-white, and cold as marble, and she couldn't take her eyes off the body curled up on the blood-wet deck. "He kept twitching," she whispered; "I wasn't sure he was dead." She crossed herself, sat down abruptly, and hung her head between her knees.

"Hi there!" McArthur's voice came faintly over the megaphone. "What's going on?"

It was Ken who was first to recover his wits. "Pete, get for'd and cut the engines." As the propellers spun to a stop, he leaned out of the hatch and shouted to *Oyster*. "We're O.K. But send over the doctor. Quick."

Scott-Henderson, unruffled as ever, was ferried to the Sea Horse. He glanced only briefly at Schultz then closed his eyes and pulled a tarpaulin over his body. But he spent a good deal longer with the unconscious Blasingame, and his voice when he at last stood up was anxious. "He's been hit damned hard on the base of the skull, probably with a pistol. When he comes round he'll need absolute quiet. And an X ray."

"That means hospital?"

"It does. And the sooner the better." He turned his attention to the girl. She seemed hardly to realize what was happening as he snapped his fingers in front of her eyes. He took Peter aside. "Her arm's O.K., but don't underestimate the danger of shock. Be gentle with her. If she's English, give her a cup of tea. If she's French or Italian, a glass of wine."

They strapped Bob Blasingame to a stretcher and ferried him carefully to the salvage vessel. He was unconscious, flushed and breathing heavily. They were laying him out in his cabin when McArthur looked in through the door. "How is he?"

"He'll live. Provided we keep him quiet."

"As bad as that! Then he'll not be flying the Sea Horse?"

Scott-Henderson looked up sharply. "He'll be lucky if he's out of bed—let alone flying—this side of Christmas."

"Hmmm! So the gold will have to stay where it is?"

Silence, as the implications of Blasingame's injury sank home. They were condemned now to the one course of action which they had wanted to avoid; they would have to make the voyage to Malta with their decks piled high with gold. And the prospect appalled them. Twice in the last few weeks they had escaped the Mafia more by luck than by judgment; they couldn't expect their luck to hold for ever. They peered through Blasingame's porthole, nervously, as though they half expected to find the sponge boats closing in.

The sea was empty and colourless. In an hour it would be dark. In a couple of hours it would be night: the hour of the hunter, and of fear.

"Of course," Peter said quietly, "*I* could fly the Sea Horse to Geneva."

Ken shook his head. "Too risky."

"Look," Peter's voice took on a familiar obstinacy. "This is just the emergency we prepared for. I did twenty hours last week in the Sea Horse, more than half of them solo. You were there on the airstrip, Ken, that afternoon when Blasingame said he'd fly with me anywhere. I wouldn't suggest it if I thought there was too much risk."

"You've not done a water takeoff. Or flown the Sea Horse at night."

"I did plenty of Walrus takeoffs in the war—as you very well know. And plenty of flying at night. The weather's perfect. If I get away the moment the boxes are loaded, the Mafia won't have a chance of spotting me in the dark. And by the time it's light I'll be letting down over Geneva."

"Hmmm!"

"Well, what's the alternative? If we head for Malta, we'll all end up with our throats cut!"

They consulted Malloy, now on oxygen-cum-neon and able to talk more or less normally. They were none of them happy with Peter's suggestion; but of several evils it struck them as being the least, and as the sun dipped into a darkening sea Malloy gave orders for the boxes of gold to be manhandled across to the Sea Horse.

It was only then that Peter had time to think of Gina.

He found her hunched up in the bow, plucking absent-mindedly at the hem of her sweater. He poured out a couple of glasses of Chianti. "Here, Gina! Drink this and you'll feel better."

She shook her head.

"It'll do you good."

She wouldn't look at him, and he saw to his embarrassment that she was crying. He put an arm awkwardly round her shoulder. "He was a bad man, Gina: a war criminal and a murderer. And if you hadn't killed him, he'd have killed you."

She muttered something in Italian.

"What was that?"

"God didn't make exceptions: He said thou shalt not kill."

It was not the remark he would have expected from a tart from the Sicilian underworld, and all his bewilderment at the role she was playing came flooding back. "Gina! How the devil did you get mixed up in this?"

She was past caring about her secret and too paid out to

dissemble; her voice was flat and disinterested. "My father," she said, "was captain of the *Selina.*"

And the bits of the jigsaw clicked into place.

Her wide-apart eyes (the first thing about her that he had noticed in the bar at Lob's Wood): he realized now of whom they had reminded him—the bearded *capitano* who had clung twenty-five years ago to the Swordfish dinghy. And her tantalizingly familiar name: hadn't Ken Richards mentioned in the garden of the hotel that the ship they had sunk was commanded by a Captain Carlo Tacchini? And, more recently, her telling him that her father had been in the Navy and that she had come to Benghazi to visit his grave.

And yet there were still things that weren't altogether clear.

She shivered.

"I'll get you a coat, Gina."

"Please. Don't leave me."

She was trembling, he realized, more with shock than cold. He held the Chianti to her lips and she sipped obediently, like a child.

"I'm sorry," she whispered, "to be silly. I haven't killed anyone before."

He remembered Scott-Henderson's warning. Somehow he had to take her mind off the shooting of Schultz. "Tell me about La Normanna, Gina."

She nestled closer. "When I was little," she said softly, "I used to help them picking the olives . . ." She talked on and on, eyes shut, in a singsong schoolgirl voice, while the moon climbed out of the sea, the stars turned blue as pinheads of acetylene, and the boxes labelled *"Specimens: Institute of Marine Biology, Geneva"* disappeared into the maw of the Sea Horse. Peter soon got a crick in his neck, and the arm on which Gina was leaning went numb with pins and needles; but he didn't move. And after about half an hour she suddenly stopped talking and opened her eyes. "Thank you, Peter. I'm O.K. now."

He fetched her a duffel-coat and they sat together in the bow, sipping cups of cocoa which the little Indonesian cook brought up from the galley. "There's a lot of things, Gina," he said slowly, "that I still don't understand."

"Such as?"

"How you came to be in Ken's flat, for instance. Why you stuck on the homing aid. And how you got into the Sea Horse."

It would be best, she told him, if she began at the beginning. And the beginning, as far as she was concerned was about six months ago.

She had just got back from America. She and her brother hadn't seen each other for a couple of years, and they decided to team up for a fortnight's holiday in North Africa. They had landed at Tripoli, hired an Alfa Romeo and set off east along the coast intending among other things to visit the ruins of Apollonia and Cyrene. After three or four days they came to Benghazi. It was their first visit to the city, and they took the opportunity to visit their father's grave. (His body had been washed ashore near the mouth of the Blue Lagoon and was buried in the El Mellaha Cemetery.) They also took the opportunity to go out in a fishing boat and have a look at the position of the *Selina.* If they had done their reconnoitering in any other week they would have come to the conclusion, like everyone else, that the merchantmen lay too deep for salvage and they would have motored on to Cyrene and taken no further part in the search for the Rommel treasure. But as luck would have it, their visit to Benghazi coincided with the preliminary survey made by Ken Richards and Gary Malloy. Gina's brother, who was a marine engineer by profession, had recognized Malloy as a leading pioneer in the field of deep-sea diving. And it wasn't hard for them to guess what had brought him to Benghazi.

It was her brother, Gina made it clear, who had thought up the somewhat harebrained scheme of their cashing in on the salvage operations. The Tacchini family, she said, had some sort of claim to part of the treasure, and they wanted to keep in touch with whoever was trying to raise it. (At this point it seemed to Peter that Gina was holding something back; but he told himself that it was hardly an auspicious moment to cross-examine her.) Luigi—her brother—had apparently suggested that they follow Ken Richards and Malloy, first during their preliminary survey and later to London. This had been comparatively easy. But what neither of them realized was that while they were shadowing Ken and Malloy, Schultz and the Mafia were shadowing them. The first hint they had of danger was when Ken was beaten up in his flat. Gina had been watching the flat at the time, and she had raised the alarm and helped to get Ken to Saint Thomas's. She had wanted, after this, to have nothing more to do with the search for the treasure; but her brother wasn't the sort to be frightened easily, and he knew even better than she how much a share of the salvage money would mean to their mother's estate.

"So," Peter's voice was thoughtful, "you followed us back to Benghazi?"

"Yes."

"And when you reckoned we were getting warm you stuck a homing aid on to *Oyster*'s hull?"

"We wanted to keep track on you, especially at night because the trawler didn't have radar. We never dreamed that as we were homing on you the Mafia were homing on us."

It was, he had to admit, all very logical. "And what happened this afternoon at the airstrip?"

Her story, once again, was convincing.

She and Luigi, she told him, had been dividing their time between watching the airfield and watching the Mafia. She had been hiding in the oil companies' hangar when the Sea Horse had come taxying up to refuel. From the shadow of the big sliding doors she had been able to see quite clearly what was going on, and after refuelling had been in progress for roughly a quarter of an hour she had spotted Schultz. He was worming his way with the skill of a professional round the blind side of a petrol bowser; a quick look back, a sudden zigzagging dash and he was scrambling undetected through the Sea Horse's cargo hatch. For perhaps a minute she had stood there irresolute, wondering what to do; then, with the idea of warning the pilot, she had started to run towards the Sea Horse's cockpit. She was halfway across the tarmac when the plane had started its engines. Afraid that it was about to taxi away she had wrenched open and tumbled in through the cargo hatch. She was lucky: a few seconds earlier and she would have landed in a heap at Schultz's feet, a few seconds later and she would have been bowled over by the slipstream as the amphibian revved up and taxied fast to the end of the runway. She lay panting on the deck of the cargo compartment: breathless, frightened and sick with pain—for as she tumbled in through the hatch she had gashed her arm. Faintly above the roar of the radials she could hear the voice of Schultz, clipped and hectoring; he was, she guessed, forcing the pilot at gunpoint to take off. With her arm streaming blood and numb from elbow to wrist, she realized she would be no match for the ex-lieutenant from the Gestapo. She looked round for somewhere to hide. And spotted the door of the inspection panel. She crawled in thankfully, closing the panel behind her.

Exactly what happened next was a matter of conjecture at the time; and it was only much later that they were able to hear the whole story from Blasingame . . . Schultz had made his plans carefully. Having hijacked the Sea Horse he had intended to force the pilot to taxi to the end of the airstrip and pick up some half-dozen of the Mafia—a strong enough posse to deal with the unsuspecting crew of the salvage vessel. But at this point his plans began to go wrong.

For Gina's brother had managed to let down the tires of the Mafia's car, so that the boarding party were stranded some two or three miles from the airfield. Peter could imagine the German's feelings as the Sea Horse waited, the minutes ticked by and his men failed to turn up at the rendezvous. Eventually the oil company became suspicious of the amphibian's behaviour and sent a car to the end of the runway to ask what she was playing at. Schultz was forced to take off in a hurry. Most men in his position would have given up; but the one-time Gestapo lieutenant lacked neither courage nor resource; he decided to hijack *Oyster* himself. And he might very well have succeeded if it hadn't been for the girl.

They were back now on ground that Peter was anxious to avoid, and Gina's hands were plucking again at the hem of her sweater. "If only," she whispered, "I hadn't killed him."

Silence, and the red and green of *Oyster*'s riding lights aglint in the sea. "It was only right," he said slowly, "that you should kill him. He killed your father."

Her eyes opened very wide. "How could you possibly know?"

He told her what had happened twenty-five years ago as their dinghy drifted waterlogged towards the Cyrenaican shore.

When he had finished she sat for a long time, very still, staring at the moonlit sea; then she gave the ghost of a smile. " 'The mills of God,' " she said, " 'grind slowly. But they grind exceedingly small.' "

He could see how it was. Blood was thicker than communion wine. She was too good a Christian to find comfort in the formula of an eye for an eye; but an eye for her father's eye—that was different.

"Hey, Pete!" Ken Richards was waving from the bridge.

He got reluctantly to his feet.

"They'll have finished loading soon. How about checking the Sea Horse?"

"Right . . . You'll be O.K., Gina?"

She nodded. "But let me do something to help. Anything."

He left her in the galley, helping "Fanny Farmer" to cut sandwiches for the flight to Geneva.

While Peter and Gina had been talking, fifty out of the sixty-odd boxes of treasure had been ferried across to the Sea Horse and secured in the hold, while Ken had worked out a detailed flight plan. But there were a number of items that Peter wanted to check for himself—the security of the boxes, the position of every control that he could possibly want to reach, and the drill for a water takeoff by night. Armed with a copy of the *Pilots' Handling Notes* he and Ken clambered into the cockpit.

The Sea Horse rode quietly at the end of her tow line, trembling and swaying faintly to the nudge of an embryo swell. It brought back memories—the two of them side by side in the cockpit, the tang of fabric and petrol and the luminous glow of instruments—and Ken's eyes as they started to run through the check list were wistful. "Wish I was coming too!"

"So do I. But it just isn't on."

"I know. But you'll need somebody with you."

His observer, he realized, was right; an extra pair of hands, no matter how unskilled, would be invaluable in helping with the radio and the ancillary controls. "I'll have a word with Gary, though God knows who he'll be able to spare . . . Hey, look at the fuel!"

They were halfway through the check list. Controls, hydraulics and the complex range of ancillaries were in order. But the fuel tanks were two-thirds empty.

Ken's voice was puzzled. "I thought he was going to top right up."

"He was interrupted." Peter gave his observer the gist of what happened at Marsa Brega.

Ken pulled a long face and tapped the fuel gauge. "Three hundred and fifty gallons. *That* won't get you to Geneva.

"Looks like I'll have to refuel. Say at Malta."

It seemed to Ken that the flight was becoming progressively less attractive. But he kept his fears to himself; the last thing he wanted was to undermine his pilot's confidence. And the rest of the checks were satisfactory.

They returned to *Oyster*; and while Ken set to work on an amended flight plan Peter discussed with Malloy the question of who—if anyone—could be spared to act as his copilot.

It was a problem. Half the crew were still incarcerated in the decompression chamber; at least two people were needed to keep a constant watch on them (controlling the gas analysers and the mass of equipment on which their lives depended); McArthur couldn't leave his bridge, the engineer couldn't leave his diesels, Scott-Henderson couldn't leave Blasingame and the divers, and Ken couldn't fly because of his injured eardrum.

"Which leaves 'Fanny Farmer' or your girl friend!"

Malloy was joking, but Peter took him seriously. "Of course. Gina's the obvious choice."

Ken Richards joined them, and they argued the moon halfway across the sky.

Malloy and Ken wouldn't hear of it at first. Only a few hours ago, they argued, they had thought the girl was one of the Mafia; it would be madness now to let her loose in a plane carrying four or five million pounds worth of gold.

"But she saved our lives." Peter was indignant. "And now we know who she is we can trust her."

"*Do* we know who she is? We've only *her* word she's Carlo Tacchini's daughter."

"You must be blind if you can't see the resemblance!"

"I dare say," Ken said quietly, "that you've observed the young lady more closely than we have." It was the nearest he ever came to telling his pilot that he thought he was making a fool of himself.

Peter looked at his watch. "Well, we'd better decide on someone. Or we'll have the Mafia cutting off our ears."

It was close on midnight; the *Citta di Livorno* had passed them over an hour ago, and there were no other ships in the vicinity.

"Doc"—Malloy's voice was almost pleading—"this is an emergency. How soon can you get me out of this chamber?"

"If you come out in the next couple of hours you'll die: painfully. If you come out in the next four hours the odds are that you'll be crippled for life with the bends. These are scientific facts, Gary. You can't escape them."

"Can't you speed things up?"

"With other men in the chamber! No."

Malloy made a last appeal. "Peter. Do you *have* to have a copilot?"

He thought carefully. "As long as things went well," he said slowly, "I *think* I could cope myself. But in an emergency—say we ran into bad weather—an extra pair of hands would probably mean the difference between life and death. And another thing. Gina used to be an air hostess. She'd be a terrific help with things like radio patter and airport procedure."

A long silence, then. "I'll talk to her. Tell her to come and sit by the decompression chamber."

Half an hour later they were ready for takeoff.

The Sea Horse and Gina had been searched, the flight plan had been checked, Malta had been alerted, and *Oyster*'s track had been laid off to Canea. (For it seemed to Malloy that by doubling back on a totally unexpected course for

Crete they would avoid any possible net that the Mafia might have cast for them.)

It was a dreamlike night as Peter and Gina were ferried across to the Sea Horse: the stars ablaze, the riding lights of ship and plane reflected in the lacquered sea, and *Oyster*'s wake a trail of phosphorescence.

"Take care of yourself, Pete." Ken's hand tightened on his pilot's shoulder, but his eyes were on the girl. She was wearing slacks and a skintight sweater, and if she had been trying to smuggle aboard even her miniature Beretta it would, he thought, have showed. "We'll keep in touch," he added, "by radio. And in forty-eight hours we'll celebrate in Geneva."

Peter nodded. He adjusted his safety belt. He pressed the starters and the Wright radials roared into life. A wave of his hand, and the tow line linking them to the familiar world of the salvage ship was cast off and they were alone in the midnight sea.

CHAPTER 13

"You know what to do?"

She nodded.

He swung the Sea Horse into wind. A final check on instruments and controls, a careful look ahead at the moonlit pathway of the sea and he eased the throttles up to and over the gate. The amphibian was slow to gather momentum, held back by friction and the weight of gold in her hull. But he didn't worry. He held the stick central to counter porpoising, let her take her time, and after a run of some mile and a quarter the vibration and the crescendo of spray subsided and she lifted cleanly into the air. At five hundred feet Gina raised the flaps. At a thousand feet she flicked the radio to transmit: "Sea Horse airborne. Height one thousand. Setting course for Malta."

"Well done," Ken's voice came through as clearly as if he were with them in the cockpit. "Keep in touch every half hour."

"Wilco." As she switched to intercom she smiled. "I told you I'd make just as good an observer as Ken."

"As good. But different."

With the tension of takeoff behind them they could relax. The Sea Horse was simple to fly, visibility was good, navigation was easy and the weather apparently set fair. Peter steadied on a course of three hundred and fifteen degrees magnetic, throttled back and trimmed the plane to fly virtually on its own. He glanced at Gina. "O.K.?"

She was leaning forward, lips parted, watching the moon transform a mass of cumulus into an ivory tower, lit as if from within by a myriad candles. She nodded. "It's beautiful."

He stared at her. "Different people have different ideas of beauty."

She didn't take her eyes off the ever-changing fabric of moon and cloud. "There's a time and place," she said, "for everything."

She wasn't, he realized, being coy: it was just that she was more interested in the magnificence of the night than in compliments. After a while he began to point out the stars: the big blue diamonds of Dubhe and Capella, the necklace of Perseus and the low-slung brooch of Boötes. And the miles slipped fast under their wing.

The weather in the central Mediterranean was not as settled as it had been in the Gulf of Sidra, and as they flew west layers of stratus began to drift wraithlike over the moon. But Peter was not worried, for already at a range of well over a hundred miles they had picked up the radio beacon at Luqa —the last time he had landed at Luqa had been in 1941 and the airfield then, he remembered, had been as cratered as no-man's-land on the Somme . . .

"How does it feel to be a millionaire?" Gina's voice cut into his thoughts.

"I've never been one," he said, "for counting chickens."

His answer seemed to amuse her. "I suppose it's being a solicitor that makes you so cautious."

"Possibly."

"Then I'll rephrase the question, m'lud. If and when you acquire the treasure what will you do with it?"

"Give ten per cent to the crew, and divide the balance equally between the three of us."

"And what will each of you do with his share?"

"Malloy is rolling already; I reckon he'll plough his back into underwater research. Ken, I just wouldn't know. He's a lone wolf and a bit of an eccentric. I wouldn't put it past him to give the bulk of it to V.S.O.: to help with his work in Tierra del Fuego."

"And you?"

"First," he said slowly, "I'll see that my children are well provided for—and that includes enough for Anne to study under the best teacher there is in Siena . . ." He came unexpectedly to a stop.

"And the rest? I suppose you'll put in some dingy old bank."

"Nonsense. I shall spend it on wine, women and song."

"What sort of women?"

He smiled at her. "Young and very attractive ones, with dark hair and blue wide-apart eyes."

To his surprise she turned away, as if embarrassed. And it occurred to him, in a moment of intuition, that there might well be an ulterior motive behind her innocent-sounding questions. "You mentioned, Gina," his voice was casual, "that your family had some sort of claim to part of the treasure?"

Her embarrassment was obvious now. "I'd rather not talk about it."

"Why on earth not?"

"The claim's only a tiny one, not worth bothering over. Forget it Peter, please."

He nodded; but a taint of the old suspicion had seeped back into their relationship.

They were halfway to Malta when the moon disappeared

behind a conglomeration of stratus. It became darker, the horizon grew blurred and Peter had to concentrate more carefully on his flying. He concentrated most on his gyro-compass and artificial horizon, taking no more than the occasional glance outside. Most of his wartime flying had been at night, and he was quite accustomed to relying on instruments alone; accustomed too to the vagaries of the mid-Mediterranean weather with its mists, *khamsins* and sudden massing of cloud—several times when his squadron had been based on Malta he had used the midnight clouds as cover from the maurauding Savoias and C.R.42s. It was, perhaps, the association of ideas that made him glance suddenly back at the Sea Horse's tail.

Fear can snowball illogically at night. It was quite impossible, he told himself, for a Mafia-controlled fighter to drop suddenly out of the cloud and on to their tail. Yet he couldn't stop himself, every now and then, glancing nervously over his shoulder. After a while Gina began to look round too. "Something the matter?"

He shook his head. He told himself not to be silly. But his fears didn't disappear, they were simply channelled into another direction. Gina had hidden in the Sea Horse: what if one of the Mafia had managed to do the same, what if one of Schultz's henchmen was at this very moment working his way towards them gun in hand? Reason told him that the idea was preposterous, for the plane had been searched. But the night was dark and the Sea Horse alive with shadows, movements and little inexplicable sounds. What, he asked himself, would he do if a gunman appeared suddenly in the cockpit? If he rammed the stick forward the man might be flung to the cabin roof, whereas he and Gina, being strapped in, would be safe. He glanced at the girl. Her safety belt lay loose in her lap. "Gina!" his voice was sharper than he realized. "Your belt!"

She snapped on the clasp. "What's wrong?"

He was about to tell her what he had been thinking, when yet another suspicion took root like a cancer in his mind. Why, he asked himself, was her belt unbuckled? Reason told him that passengers in aircraft often unbuckled their belts, that it was more comfortable this way; but he couldn't help wondering if she might perhaps have a not-so-innocent motive, the wish to be free to help whoever was creeping up from the tail of the plane. He told himself the idea was absurd and contemptible, and he would never have thought of it if he hadn't been piqued by her making a mystery out of her family's claim to the treasure. But his fears refused to subside. People, he reminded himself cynically, would do *anything* to get their hands on gold worth four to five million pounds. And the night grew darker and the hold of the Sea Horse increasingly alive with an indefinable menace. He flew on, cocooned in cloud, cold and trembling with a fear that for all its illogicality he couldn't dam back. Soon they would be approaching Sicily, the traditional stamping ground of the Mafia. Here if anywhere the hijacking would be attempted. "Gina," his voice was strained; "time to contact *Oyster*."

There was no reply. And looking down at her he saw that she was asleep.

For a moment he couldn't believe it. Then relief flooded over him. No one—not even the most hardened of the Mafia—would be likely to drop asleep if they knew that the plane in which they were flying was about to be hijacked.

They flew on through the humid mosaic of mist and cloud, homing straight as pigeon to cote on the Luqa beacon.

He didn't wake Gina until they were approaching the airfield.

An anaemic sun was struggling out of the sea as they made contact with the airport control. Flying conditions were none too easy, and he was glad of Gina's help with the radio. "Hello, Luqa Tower. This is Bolus Sea Horse on unscheduled flight. We are overhead at three thousand feet. Request landing instructions."

"Roger, Sea Horse. You are clear to descend. Runway two-four. Visibility eight hundred yards. Call finals."

A whisper from Peter.

"Repeat visibility, Luqa."

"Eight hundred yards. Low cloud and mist. Thickening. If you want to divert to Sicily, Catania is clear."

They exchanged glances: the last place they wanted to end up in was Sicily. They told the controller they were coming in.

Peter checked the length of the runway: 7,800 feet: nearly three times the length in which the Sea Horse ought to pull up. To an experienced pilot it would be easy; but he had to admit he would have been a great deal happier if the airfield had been in the clear. He let down carefully, running twice through the pre-landing check list. Everything, as far as he could tell, was in order—though he was surprised at how long it took for the undercarriage to lock into place. He was down to eight hundred feet before they broke cloud and saw beneath them the patchwork of green and ochre fields. But of the airfield there was no sign. He nodded to Gina.

"Sea Horse finals."

"Sea Horse clear to land."

He was beginning to think he had misjudged the run-in when he saw, dead ahead, the golden glow of the approach lights. "Forty-degree flap." He saw out of the corner of his eye Gina's hand tighten on the lever, but it seemed an eternity before the drag took effect and his airspeed dropped. They were, he realized, coming in too high and too fast. He pulled back the throttles; he pushed down the nose, and the runway came flowing up at them like a great grey river in spate. As he levelled off, the lights swung into line, his wheels drummed, his brakes squealed and they were lurching fast over the mist-wet tarmac. It was not an elegant landing; but they were down.

Following directions from Luqa control, he taxied towards a hangar in the northwest corner of the airfield. He was halfway round the perimeter track when Ken's voice came over the radio—now they were at ground level they had to turn the volume to maximum to hear what he was saying. "Hello, Sea Horse: are you safely down?"

"Hello, *Oyster*: down in one piece!"

"Well done. Listen, Pete, you may have difficulty in getting away from Luqa. We've been checking on the weather and it's not too good. If you *have* to stay, don't whatever you do unload the marine specimens."

"Right."

"Now Malloy and I have arranged for a couple of chaps to meet you: a Flight Lieutenant Jardine and a Willis Coulson. Jardine is aide to the A.O.C., and Coulson is an ex-driller —a good man to have on your side if it comes to a scrap. You can trust them a hundred per cent. And they'll give you a hand with taking care of the Sea Horse."

"Right again. But how can I recognize them and check their *bona fide*?"

When Ken had given him all the information he needed Peter taxied clear of the perimeter track and up to a solid well-guarded hangar. He locked the brakes, shut down the engines and helped Gina out of the plane.

An R.A.F. van was parked in front of the hangar, and a sandy-haired flight lieutenant came forward to meet them. "Mr. Peter Grey?"

"That's me."

"My name's Jardine." (He had guessed as much from Ken's description.) "The A.O.C. sends his compliments, and he's asked me to give you any help you need."

"Very kind of you both. Can I introduce Signorina Tacchini?"

"Boun giorno, signorina . . . I'm afraid I've bad news. There's a hell of a storm over Italy, and northbound flights are cancelled."

Peter swore softly. "We'd hoped to refuel and be off. We don't want to leave the plane."

"I know all about your marine specimens! May I make a suggestion?" Jardine pointed to the hangar. "That's the bonded warehouse. If you park the Sea Horse there she'll be ninety-nine per cent safe. And to make that a hundred per cent I can fix an R.A.F. guard. Why not leave the plane there while you have a word with the meteorological people. You might persuade them to let you go."

He was hesitating when Gina laid a hand on his arm. "Would you like me to stay with the Sea Horse?"

It was said with an innocent smile. But suspicion once roused dies hard. He turned to Jardine. "If you fix the guard," he said slowly, "I'd like a word with whoever's in charge. Then we can all go to the met office together."

The guard turned out to be everything he had hoped for; a dozen A.C.2s under the command of a tough-looking flight sergeant; and within half an hour of their landing, the Sea Horse was bolted and barred in the bonded warehouse under the surveillance of both airport police and the R.A.F.

But the weather was not dealt with so easily.

"There's a front moving east over Italy," the controller told them. "Heavy rain, poor visibility and cloud right down to the deck. As for getting into Geneva, you haven't a hope. In this sort of weather the Alps are an absolute death trap. Even the transcontinental jets are being diverted."

"When'll the front clear?"

"It's moving fast. The cloud ought to start lifting during the night, and with any luck conditions'll be O.K. by the morning."

Peter's foot tapped impatiently on the marbled floor. "How about a takeoff late this evening: say five o'clock?"

"Not a hope in hell. Not even for scheduled flights."

It was no good, he realized, kicking against the pricks. They were trapped and there was nothing they could do about it. They could only hope that the weather would clear before the Mafia caught up with them.

Jardine and Coulson both offered their hospitality; but Peter decided it would be best if he and Gina booked into a hotel in Valletta.

Their feelings as they took a cab into the city were mixed: anxiety at having to leave the Sea Horse, frustration at being held up with the gold only a few hours' flight from the vaults of the Banque Helvétia, exhaustion—they had neither of them enjoyed much sleep in the previous forty-eight hours—and underneath it all a growing tendency for their eyes to keep meeting and then look quickly away. As they booked into the Phoenicia, Peter couldn't help thinking wryly that it was not two single rooms that 007 would have asked for.

The Phoenicia was both balm and aphrodisiac: cool marble, thick-piled carpets and the sophisticated service to delight a cosmopolitan élite. As they sipped coffee under the palms of a sun-warmed courtyard they relaxed and talked of what they ought to do next.

Gina wanted more than anything to sleep: to sleep and forget, as far as she could, the bullet-torn body of Schultz; and the dark circles under her eyes made Peter conscious of just how much she had been through in the last few hours. He took her hand. "You have a couple of aspirin and a good long rest."

She smiled at him gratefully. "And what'll *you* do?"

"Get my head down too. And keep a check on the Sea Horse."

"And, I hope, shave!" Her fingers brushed his cheek. "I'm sorry to be a bore. I'll be better company this evening, I promise."

"I'll look forward," he said, "to this evening."

When she had gone up the cool marble stairs to her room, he felt very much alone.

The morning and afternoon passed slowly.

He shaved and showered and lay on his bed and tried to sleep but sleep wouldn't come because he was worried about the plane, and after a snack lunch in the Pegasus Bar he took a cab to the airfield to check that the guards were on the *qui vive.* They were. And he found to his satisfaction that he couldn't get within a hundred yards of the hangar without being challenged by men with Alsatians and sub-machine guns.

Back in the hotel, acting on a sudden impulse, he put through an international telephone call to his family; and the sound of Anne's voice brought him back to a world that had once seemed drab and unexciting but which now in retrospect appeared wonderfully stable and safe. He kept her on the line for more than half an hour, drinking in all that she and the little ones had been doing. She wasn't used to such extravagance. "Hadn't you better ring off, Daddy? This call must be costing a fortune!"

"I've a fortune," he said slowly, "to spare. You needn't worry now about Siena."

She sounded frightened. "Be careful, please." A pause, and a sudden breathlessness in her voice. "We none of us care about Siena. We just want you back."

He was touched more deeply than he cared to show: "I'll be back all right, I hope in a couple of days. My love to Wendy and Richard."

"And ours to you."

As he put down the receiver he felt happy and relaxed: it was good to remind himself of how much the Rommel treasure would mean to his family.

After an early tea, thinking that Gina had slept long enough, he climbed to the second floor and knocked on the door of her suite. There was no reply. He was about to ask reception to give her a call, when almost as an afterthought he tried the door. To his surprise it was unlocked. He walked in, and the first thing he saw was the empty bed.

For a second he could think of only two possibilities: either she had been kidnapped or she had gone to contact the Mafia. Then he became aware of the splashing of water and the clothes laid neatly out on a chair by her bed. She was only having a bath.

The splashing stopped: *"Qui è?"* Her voice was frightened.

"It's me. Peter."

"Oh!" He could sense her relief. "What a time to come in. I've nothing on."

He sat on the edge of the bed. "I'm broadminded."

A pause; then a hand appeared briefly round the bathroom door. "A gentleman would bring me my clothes."

He considered what was on the chair; then picked up and carried over her sandals.

"That isn't fair!"

"All's fair," he said, "in love and war."

"And which are you playing at?"

Playing at, he told himself, was right: it was only a game, a delightfully sophisticated game, it is true, but nothing more. And yet the witty reply that was on the tip of his tongue felt suddenly cheap, and he was conscious of a feeling of tenderness that he hadn't experienced for more years than he cared to admit. "We're not enemies," he said slowly, "so there's no need for us to fight any more. And I'm not playing a game."

A long pause, then her face appeared round the bathroom door. "Say that last bit again."

"I said I'm not playing a game."

She came uncertainly into the bedroom, draped in the most enormous royal blue towel that might have been dyed to match her eyes. "What are you trying to tell me, Peter?"

He kissed her. For a moment the memory of other lips was

an almost physical barrier; then, under the darting sweetness of her tongue, all that was past was forgotten.

When he dropped his arms, she was trembling. "You'd better go. Please."

He hesitated. "But this is the time and place you were talking about: for everything."

"Please, Peter. Please go."

There was an indecision in her eyes that he didn't understand. He was not much of a psychologist, but he could sense that it wasn't the physical act of love she was frightened of; it was something else; some barrier that she couldn't bring herself to cross. A younger or less perceptive man might have been misled by the classic stage props of seduction: by the panties and bra on the back of the chair, and her long bare legs still warm from the bath disappearing into the folds of the towel. But he was watching her eyes. And what he saw made him draw back. He reached for the handle of the door. "If you'll put on something a bit more conventional," he said, "I suggest we go out and paint the town."

She smiled uncertainly: "Give me an hour to shop, and I'll be with you."

She was a good deal longer than an hour, but when she eventually knocked on the door of his suite he had to admit the wait was well worthwhile. She was wearing bell bottom hipsters of sapphire blue, black boots and a jacket of sapphire, black and white. She pirouetted in front of him with a sort of determined gaiety. "And which bit of town do we paint first?"

They went first of all to the airfield for yet another check that the Sea Horse would be doubly guarded during the night; and when they saw the sort of security that Coulson had laid on, they set off with easy consciences for Sliema.

It was a pleasant evening: a fresh wind tumbling banks of nut-brown cumulus over the darkening sky, and the promenades alive with the slap of waves and the twinkling lights of restaurants and bars. They strolled along with the crowds, admiring the yachts in the marina, the rose-gold stone of the forts, and the dexterity of the fishermen mending their nets. On the surface they were full of *camaraderie,* but underneath there was tension.

After a while they climbed down the rocks to a sheltered sea-water pool where a handful of enthusiasts were bathing. As they watched the swimmers he turned to her with a smile. "Pity you haven't brought your bikini."

"You've a one-track mind," she said. And she said it without enthusiasm.

Ever since he had kissed her she had been preoccupied and restrained. In Benghazi it had been she who had made all the running; but now that he was beginning to respond she seemed to be backing out. Yet it would be a facile judgment, his instinct told him, to dub her a tease. Perhaps, he thought wryly, his kiss had brought home the fact that he was old enough to be her father.

A tanker moved slowly along the horizon, the ruby glow of its light still visible long after the vessel itself had disappeared; clouds rolled over the moon, the wind sighed softly in from the sea and Gina shivered.

"Dinner?"

She nodded.

The Draget Restaurant was cool and plush and intimate: grey stone walls and polished woodwork, fresh flowers and subtly shaded lights; Gina was the prettiest girl in the room, and the *truites du lac* and the Chianti Ruffino were everything that could have been asked for. But the meal was not, to start with, a success.

"What's bothering you, Gina?"

She drained and held out her glass. "Don't," she said, "ask questions. Just enjoy your wine and your woman."

He filled her glass. "How can I: when my woman isn't enjoying herself?"

She swore softly in Italian.

"Which being translated means?"

For a moment she hesitated, her fingers tight round the stem of her glass; then, as if suddenly making up her mind, she leaned forward smiling. "Mr. Grey," she said, "would you please behave like everyone else and stare at my breasts or my legs. Not my eyes?"

"But I like to stare at all three."

"My eyes," she said, "are private property. Is it necessary that I put up a little notice 'not for sale'?"

He got the implication: that the notice applied to her eyes only. "Why don't you stop putting on an act, Gina? And just tell me what's the matter?"

"Your eyes, Mr. Grey! Please don't make things *too* difficult."

He lowered his sights the requisite eight or nine inches, and her voice took on a brittle gaiety that he didn't like. "Have you read a book called *On Her Majesty's Secret Service*?"

"James Bond?"

"Yes."

He nodded.

"You remember that droll little scene in the Casino? Where he bought the girl for a couple of million francs?"

"I wouldn't have put it quite like that. But I know the bit you mean."

She eyed him, tongue between teeth, over the rim of her glass. "She was a cheap little piece. *My* price is ten million lira."

He stared at her. "And worth every penny, I'm sure. But I've not the slightest idea what you're talking about."

"Of course you haven't. But I'll tell you. I'll be very, how do you say, implicit." She drank her Chianti in a single gulp, folded her hands in her lap and stared straight through him. "I'll begin at the beginning: immediately after the war: when the Navy tried to salvage the *Selina* . . . A lot of father's friends, you must understand, were in the Ministry of Marine, and, because of his war record and the commandeering of our estate, they agreed to give our family one per cent of the salvage money. It was all very legal with documents and signatures and sealing wax by the litre. One per cent of the salvage money would have brought in more than ten million lira, and that would have put La Normanna nicely back on its feet. So you can imagine how mother felt when the salvage failed. Next year there was another attempt. Again we were promised one per cent. And again the salvage failed. There was a third attempt—I think in 1957—with the same promise and the same result. Then, years later, you turned up. I said to Luigi, 'Let's ask these people if *they'll* give us one per cent as well.' I remember his reply: 'They didn't know father, they aren't Italian, and why should they hand over more than ten million lira for nothing?' So we agreed to watch you and see what would happen. Luigi thought it would help if I got friendly with you." His lips tightened. "Oh, don't look so damned disapproving! I know it makes him sound like a pimp, but he only wanted me to find out your plans and lead you up the garden path . . . Well," her eyes were defiant, "whatever else I do I don't lead people up the garden path. At least not people I'm fond of. And like Luigi, I don't expect to be given something for nothing."

He moistened his lips; he wasn't sure even now if he'd got the message. "Are you offering to sleep with me in return for one per cent of the Rommel treasure?"

"Yes."

He stared at her. "You value yourself very highly!"

He thought that her eyes would drop, but they didn't. "I promise to do my best," she said, "to give you good value."

His throat felt suddenly dry. He topped up their glasses, and knocked his back at a single gulp. It was her idea. And he would barely miss ten million lira. He thought of the warmth of her body and the softness of her lips. Their eyes met.

It was the eyes that decided him. She was smiling, and her lips were carefully moistened and parted in the approved sex-kitten style; but the eyes that stared into his were cold as agate. This was a business proposition. "No," he said, "that's not the way I want it."

She blinked once, otherwise she made not the slightest move. Her voice was dead. "Will you please take me back to the hotel."

"When I've explained how I feel."

"There's nothing to explain. I understand." She pushed back her chair.

"Please, Gina. I don't think you understand at all. If the Italian government thought you deserved a rake-off, that's good enough for me. You can have it. Without any strings."

She sat down, bewildered. "You do not wish to make love to me?"

"Of course I do. But I don't want to buy you."

She stared at him: for a long time. Then she said slowly. "Not many Italian men would have kissed me as you kissed me, then turned such an offer down."

"A pity I'm not Italian."

She continued to stare at him as though he were some strange creature whose existence she couldn't bring herself to believe in. "So you'll give me ten million lira for nothing? Just like that?"

"You *did* save our lives, remember. Besides there'll be enough for everyone."

She smiled an uncertain smile. "You are very sweet, Peter. And your gift will bring great happiness to my mother." The words were trite, polite and impersonal. For a moment they stared at one another, then the façade broke and she buried her face in her hands, sobbing soundlessly, the tears running warm through her fingers and on to the lace-edged tablecloth.

After a while he passed her his handkerchief.

"I'm sorry," she whispered. "It's over now." She blew her nose and reached for his hand, and the constraint that had built up between them ebbed suddenly away, like a flood tide with the wind behind it ripping fast over the mud flats of an estuary. He ordered another bottle of Chianti, and they relaxed and ate their *truites du lac* and laughed and danced and were more at ease with one another than they had ever been in Benghazi.

And yet one thing that had added spice to their relationship in North Africa was missing now. She didn't flirt with him. That, she told herself, would hardly be fair.

She broke her new-made resolution only once: in the taxi that was taking them back to the Phoenicia. Then, with her hand in his and her head resting lightly against his shoulder, she said without looking up. "Were you just a little bit tempted?"

"More than just a little bit. As you very well know!"

She closed her eyes and smiled.

There were still a fair number of people about as the taxi dropped them at the steps leading up to the hotel. At the entrance to the foyer, Gina paused. "Will you be wanting me tomorrow?"

"But of course"—he had taken it for granted that she would be flying with him to Geneva.

"Sure you don't want a copilot, or a navigating officer or whatever they're called? I'm sure your R.A.F. would provide one."

"I want *you*. The less outsiders involved in this the better. Besides, we're partners now."

"Business partners, at any rate." Her hand tightened suddenly on his: so tightly that he almost cried out. "Pete! In here." She pulled him quickly into the dark little courtyard where not many hours earlier they had drunk their coffee. Her voice was shaking; her face in the light of the moon was white as chalk. "That man by the desk. He's one of the Mafia."

From the dimly lit entrance to the courtyard they peered at the figure sitting placidly behind the *Malta Times*: middle-aged, thick-set, sallow-skinned, in a dark anonymous suit: he might have been any watcher in any hotel anywhere in the world.

"Are you sure?"

She nodded. "I saw him in Benghazi. And again at the airstrip. Oh, Pete: I thought all that was over."

"It won't be over," he said slowly, "till the gold's lying safe in the vaults of the Banque Helvétia."

They stared at the squat impassive figure like birds at a snake. They would have to walk past him to reach the lifts; but there were stairs at the opposite end of the foyer. They thought that he had almost certainly seen them, and they were not quite sure why they didn't walk openly past him; but it suddenly seemed important that they should get to their rooms without being spotted. They tiptoed through the palm-dark courtyard, came quietly into the far end of the foyer and stole conspiratorlike up the stairs.

The *Malta Times* neither rustled nor moved.

At the entrance to their suites they paused. They looked at each other. Gina was trembling. She reached for his hand. "I'm sorry. I'm frightened."

"Have you got the key to your room?"

She felt in her bag, and her eyes opened very wide. "I must have left it at the desk."

He unlocked and held open his door. "Come on," he said. "I'll see that you don't get hurt."

CHAPTER 14

He turned the key in the lock. He closed and bolted the windows. He checked that the door to the adjoining suite was secure. "Now nobody," he said, "can get in."

"And I can't get out."

Their eyes kept meeting, and with a sense of frank enjoyment that would not under different circumstances have been there. He reached for the telephone. "Business," he said, "before pleasure."

He made three calls. The first to Jardine to warn the guard to be especially on the alert, the second to Coulson to arrange for the Mafia's watchdog to be removed from the foyer, and the third to room service to order *"deux café complet"* for eight in the morning.

Halfway through the first of the calls Gina disappeared into the bathroom. He had been vaguely conscious while phoning, of the sound of the shower and the scent of soap and the warmth of steam through the half-open door. Now, as he undressed in silence and turned out all but the bedside light, he was even more conscious of the hundred and one little movements and sounds that reminded him of her nearness: the gurgle of water as she sluiced down the shower, the pad of bare feet on marble tiles, and the brush of the towel over her body. "Can I borrow your toothbrush?" she called.

"Of course."

The trickling of water in the basin and the scrub of nylon against her teeth.

"And your pajamas?"

"Most certainly not!"

A pause, then her head appeared round the bathroom door. "I don't imagine you go in for Diorissimo?"

"Sorry. Only Corvette After Shave."

"Then I suppose," she said, "I won't be able to wear anything tonight."

As she came half-shy and half-provocative into the circle of lamplight he thought that no woman in the world, not even Jean, could have looked more beautiful. He reached for her. And the things that had for years been dammed back began to break loose in a slow triumphant flood.

It would be wrong to say that he had forgotten how wonderful making love could be; rather he had forced himself to forget. But he remembered that night, remembered and learned anew.

He woke suddenly and all-of-a-piece. The light was grey and a dawn wind was moaning softly in from the sea. He heard Gina beside him catch her breath; he felt her trembling. "Hey, what's the matter?"

She clung to him like a shocked child. "Oh, Pete! Thank God you're here."

He held her close. "Where did you think I was?"

"I had a dream." As she switched on the lamp her voice was shaking. "Just checking it's really you!"

He ran a hand through her hair. "It's me. And the dream's over."

She nodded, but it was some time before she stopped trembling.

"Would it help to tell me?"

She moistened her lips. "There was a river, a great black river in flood. And a current that swept us away. And I was sort of pinned down and couldn't swim."

"We'll have to be careful where we go bathing!"

"And a terrible old man in a rowing boat. He just sat there and watched and didn't help."

He remembered the nightmare that had haunted him twenty-five years ago in the hospital in Tripoli. "What sort of man?"

"All in black. I couldn't see his face."

He remembered as though it were yesterday his hours of delirium on the banks of the River Styx, and the fisherman in his *gaiassa* who had got mixed up in his mind with the Charon of the ancient Greeks for whose passengers there was no return. And he shivered.

She pulled up the eiderdown. "Now you're trembling!"

He told himself it was only a dream: a silly meaningless dream. He took her in his arms. He kissed her almost desperately to silence: kissed her as though some instinct warned him that he might never have the chance of kissing her again.

Later, when she was pouring their coffee, he ran a finger thoughtfully down her spine. "Darling!"

"Hmmm!"

"Will you marry me?"

Her eyes opened very wide. "You don't have to, you know. Just because you've slept with me."

"I know that."

"We'd probably have children . . ."

"Very probably, I'd say!"

"You wouldn't mind their being Catholics?"

"Other things being equal," he said slowly, "I'd have preferred my children brought up in the Church of England. But you have to promise. And so that's all there is to it."

"But you wouldn't hold it against me? Or them?"

"So long," he said, "as they're brought up as Christians, I can't see it's all that important."

For a moment she looked at him very straight, then she slipped out of bed. She curtsied. "Your kind invitation, sir, is accepted with pleasure. In fact"—as he held out his arms—"with very much pleasure indeed."

It was not until later, as they were dressing, that he noticed that during the night her handbag had slipped off the chair by the bed. Its contents lay strewn on the thick-piled carpet: lipstick, compact, handkerchief, and the key to her room.

He felt flattered at the time: astonished and grateful for her deception. But later, as they were waiting for a cab to take them to the airport, she said something that made him ask himself if there mightn't perhaps be more to her deception than met the eye.

"Peter!"

"Hmmm?"

Her voice was thoughtful. "Why are you so keen to get the gold to Geneva?"

"It's a question of tax."

"Couldn't we bank it here in Malta?"

"We could. But we'd have to pay a crippling duty on it."

"Even so, we'd be left with a small fortune?"

"Only about a million."

"Isn't a million enough?"

He looked at her curiously. "What are you getting at, Gina?"

She reached for his hand. "I know it sounds silly. But we've got so much. Here. In the bag. So much that's ours for the taking. Without any more risk. We've got each other and something like three or four hundred thousand pounds. Why be greedy and want more?"

"So?"

"Why not leave the gold where it is and fly to Brindisi and get married?"

He was often to ask himself later why in God's name he hadn't agreed. Part of the reason was obvious: two-thirds of the gold wasn't his to decide what to do with. But there was more to it than that. And he was too honest not to torture himself with the truth. He loved Gina, that was true, but his love was far from perfect. He asked her to be his wife, to share his life and to bear his children, and yet he didn't completely trust her, so that even now as they sat in the elegant lounge of the Phoenicia a nightmare scene began to build up in his mind, of his stammered excuses to Ken and Malloy, "She said why don't we get married and how was I to know that on our way to the church her friends the Mafia were going to steal the gold?" "But Gina," he said slowly, "what would Ken and Malloy have to say? It's their gold as much as ours. And anyhow it's not worth throwing away two or three million pounds, just to get married a day earlier!"

"I suppose not."

He took her hand. "We'll get married the moment the gold's in the vaults of the Banque Helvétia. Tomorrow."

"Domani e domani e domani!" She shivered. Then, with a determined change of mood, she gave him a smile. "Forget it. You ought to be flattered your fiancée can hardly wait!"

Her quick acquiescence made his suspicions seem all the more contemptible. For a second he was tempted to play it her way: to fly with her to Brindisi or anywhere else in the world that she wanted to fly to: to grab the happiness that they had in hand and have nothing further to do with the Rommel gold. Then the *concierge* was coming towards them between the sun-flecked palms. "Your taxi to the airport, sir."

They were met in flying control by a somewhat harassed Jardine. A couple of light privately owned Fiats, the aide told them, had flown in less than an hour ago from Catania. There hadn't been anything about the Fiats that was overtly suspicious, only the faintest aura of mystery.

"You think they're the Mafia's?" Peter was disbelieving.

"They *could* be planning an interception, say over Sicily. But we'll soon put a stop to that."

It was a simple but effective plan that Jardine outlined. Step one, the Fiats would be prevented taking off until well after the Sea Horse had left. Step two, Peter's flight plan would specify his route as first crossing Sicily and then following the Italian coast via Naples and Rome; but he would in fact fly by a very different track, well to the west *via* Sardinia and Corsica. This, Peter agreed, made sense. He didn't believe that an interception was even remotely on the cards: that sort of thing, he told himself, simply didn't happen in real life. But there was no harm in taking precautions: by following Jardine's suggestion they would be underwriting success.

They took off at half-past nine, with the light now bright, now muted as the sun chased cotton-wool clouds round the kaleidoscope of the sky.

He thought that everything was neatly tied up. The Sea Horse had been refuelled; she had been searched by the R.A.F. Police, and he had checked personally that the gold was still in the boxes. There was nothing now, he told himself, that could stop them.

His confidence suffered a momentary jolt within seconds of takeoff. As the Sea Horse lifted clear of the runway, he nodded at Gina: "Undercarriage."

She selected "undercarriage up" and nothing happened.

"Undercarriage!" His voice was sharp; for he could tell by the drag that the wheels had failed to retract.

"But I *have* pulled the lever!"

He looked quickly sideways at the wings and saw to his relief that the wheels were rising. But slowly. It was a couple of minutes from the time Gina selected the control to the time the indicator lights flickered from red to green. And the same thing happened when it came to raising the flaps. They swung up; they locked into place; but with nerve-racking reluctance. He felt a stir of unease. Could he, he asked himself, be doing something wrong; or was the fault in the plane? He wished now that he had had her serviced—Jardine had suggested this, but he knew that she had been given an intermediate inspection at Marsa and it had seemed wisest not to have a whole crowd of mechanics swarming over the boxes of gold. Gina was watching him anxiously. "Everything O.K.?"

He reached for her hand. "Everything's fine. Can you get us cleared for Geneva?"

She switched the radio to transmit. "Bolus Sea Horse to Luqa. We are at eight thousand feet, setting course for Geneva *via* Naples and Rome. Thank you for looking after us."

"Roger, Sea Horse. Good day and good trip."

He synchronized the engines at a hundred and fifty knots and adjusted the trim tabs. The Wright radials purred sweetly and reassuringly, the controls were light and precise, the dials of the instruments were at normal, and his embryo fears—which had never in any case been more than a whisper—subsided into the limbo of things that it was not too difficult to forget.

It was a beautiful morning for flying: strong light, unlimited visibility, and a tumult of puffy white clouds scudding east in the wake of the depression. They headed first for Sicily; but once out of sight of the airfield they lost height and altered course to the west. Soon they were passing low over the volcanic cone of Pantelleria, its rocks white with seagull droppings and spray; then they spotted Tunisia, the promontory of Cape Bon delineated sharply in the glare of the morning sun. There was no sign of pursuit.

Gina was like a little girl at a carnival. "This is better

than carrying round the dinner trays at thirty-five thousand!"

"Flying below cloud is fun; there's always masses to see. Look! A couple of Nato destroyers and a helicopter."

"Can *we* have a plane?"

He sighed in mock despair. "I see my new wife will soon drive me to the poorhouse!"

She shook her head. "I don't want a great big house. Or mink or pearls. But a plane would be fab—you could teach me to fly"

He opened his signal pad. "We'll make a list of things to take on our honeymoon. One plane."

"No, one seaplane. Then we can bathe from it."

"Right. One seaplane, one crate of beer."

"Heaven help me," she said, "I'm marrying a dipsomaniac. One bikini."

"That's two items, not one."

"And which item, sir, will you allow me to bring?"

"Let me think now"—his eyes admired her—"what a delightful choice to have to make . . ."

By the time the cloud-ringed hills of Sardinia appeared over the horizon they had covered two sides of the signal pad.

It was siesta time in Sardinia, fields and woods and golden sands asleep in the warmth of the sun; nothing moved as they flew low over the fairy-tale coast—except once when a cloud of black and white gulls rose wheeling in protest from an outcrop of rock.

And so to Corsica, with its more rugged cliffs and darker forests. They were halfway now to the vaults of the Banque Helvétia; the Sea Horse was eating away the miles with a contented purr; there was no sign of the Mafia; and Peter and Gina, cocooned in the womb of the plane, were at peace with the world, each other and themselves. They were approaching the Ajaccio Beacon when she asked him about his family.

"Let's see if I've got them right: Anne seventeen, Richard ten and Wendy six?"

"Right. Have you seen their photos?"

She shook her head.

Holding the control column with his left hand, he fumbled for his wallet. "That's Anne."

"Hmmm! She looks a sweetie. She's got your mouth."

"You'll take to each other, I know. And these are the little ones."

"You've a good-looking family."

He was putting the photos away when the plane lurched awkwardly in a down draught and the wallet slid off his lap and on to the deck plates. As Gina picked it up she noticed another much older photograph sandwiched between the liras and Libyan pounds. "Is this Jean?"

He nodded.

She looked at the photograph carefully, for a long time. "She was beautiful, Peter."

"I've been lucky," he said, "with all my wives. . . . I suppose," he added hesitantly, "I shouldn't be carrying her photo about with me now."

"Why ever not?"

"You don't mind?"

She looked at him curiously. "You ask me to marry you, but you don't *really* know me, do you!"

"A lot of women wouldn't like it, I know that."

"I'm not a lot of women. Listen, I read a book once by one of your English novelists. The heroine had been married before, and in the last chapter when she'd got herself a new husband she picked up the photo of the first husband who'd died and kissed it and swore she'd put it away in the bottom of a drawer and never look at it again, and I thought oh my God how terrible for that poor first husband to be pushed away in a drawer and forgotten, like a pile of dust one pretends isn't there and sweeps under a carpet—I shouldn't think Jean would like to be swept away like a pile of dust."

It was his turn now to look at her curiously. "Aren't you afraid I'll be reminded of her? On the days when everything goes wrong? And that I'll make comparisons?"

"Look," she said, "be realistic. If I *don't* make you happy, you'll hanker after her, photo or no photo. If I *do* make you happy, why should I want you to forget her?"

He stared at her. "You know what I like about you most. You've got courage."

She smiled. "Let's say I'm not afraid of a gamble. When I fancy the odds."

"What *are* you afraid of, Gina?"

"Are we being serious?"

He nodded.

"There're only two things," she said slowly, "that *really* frighten me."

"Which are?"

"Being crippled. And death."

It was not quite the answer he had expected. "Being crippled I can understand. But death—I mean surely as a Christian . . . ?"

"Oh, of course," her fingers moved to her crucifix, "I believe in the resurrection of the body, and the life everlasting. That goes without saying. But life on earth's so wonderful, especially now, I just don't want it to end. As for being crippled: cripples are so dependent, aren't they? Such a nuisance to other people."

"Hmmm!"

He realized that the Ligurian Sea was behind them and ahead lay the maritime alps of Provence, climbing in ochre olive and purple tiers to the northern skyline. They were on the last leg now, coming up to the final run-in. Another hour and the affair of the Rommel treasure would be over and done with: there would be an end to danger and excitement, and he could settle down to the familiar and worthwhile joys of family life: with Gina.

They flew up the valley of the Rhône on the classic approach route to Geneva, the route which privately operated aircraft usually followed to circumnavigate the Alps. Here, it seemed to Peter, among the foothills of the Vaucluse was the Mafia's last opportunity to intercept them. But his instinct reiterated that no interception would take place. It might have been different if Schultz had lived. But the Gestapo lieutenant lay weighted in canvas under a thousand feet of Mediterranean sea, and the men he had worked with lacked his fanaticism; they were professionals; given half a chance they would still make a grab for the treasure—witness their tailing the Sea Horse as far as Luqa—but they wouldn't, Peter felt sure, stick out their necks in a lost cause: and that the forcing down of the Bolus in broad daylight would certainly be.

Never, he thought as he flew up the valley, had the world looked so beautiful; the silver snake of the river winding through terraced vineyards, the green of the pines and the random splashes of gold where birch and mulberry cascaded over the limestone scarps, and all washed clean and scented sweet by yesterday's rain. There, he told himself, was the place to be; not high in the too-bright sky, nor low in the too-dark sea, but rooted firm to the surface of the earth that had been man's home for countless millions of years. This is what he and Gina would settle down to: ordinary simple life. He had drunk his fill of adventure.

Soon they could see the snow-white peaks of the Alps; the mass of Mont Blanc and away in the distance the more slender spire of the Matterhorn.

It would be hard to say exactly how, when or why he caught the first faint whiff of danger. Certainly there was no specific occurrence that made him aware of it; and yet by the time they sighted the Lake of Geneva he was very much on the alert. He had, as a pilot, a better-than-average nose for trouble; a flair for looking up at the right moment to spot the Macchi diving out of the sun, a knack of picking the one landing out of a hundred on which to disregard the wave of the batsman's arms. And he felt now, more strongly than ever in his life, the ambiance of fear: the premonition of disaster. It was illogical. The Sea Horse was flying perfectly. His instruments were at normal. And yet for a reason that he couldn't begin to account for he could feel little beads of moisture aprick at his palms. He took the precaution that was to save his life: "Gina!"

"Hmmm!"

"Let's have the *Pilots' Handling Notes.*"

She passed him the little blue booklet. "Nothing wrong, is there?"

He shook his head. "Just checking the landing drill. You call Geneva while I have a look at the book of words."

She switched the radio to transmit. "Hello, Geneva Control. This is Bolus Sea Horse on unscheduled flight. We are forty miles southwest at eight thousand feet. Request approach instructions."

"Hello, Bolus Sea Horse. You are clear to descend to Sottons Beacon, for straight approach on to runway two-three. Call at beacon."

"Roger, Geneva."

"Right." Peter handed her the *Notes.* "Now I want to do a dummy landing at eight thousand feet. Let's imagine we're on the final approach and coming in to the runway. If you read out the checks, I'll operate the controls. O.K.?"

She nodded. "But everything's all right, isn't it?"

"I think so. But if there *is* something wrong I'd rather know at eight thousand than eight hundred. The checks start there."

She placed her finger at the top of the list. "Autopilot out."

"Right."

"Auxiliary fuel pumps on."

"Right."

"Propellers in fine pitch."

He adjusted the pitch control. "Right."

"Lower undercarriage."

He pulled back the lever. "Right."

"Check visually and on indicators that undercarriage is locked in place."

They could see the wheels subsiding out of the wing roots. Slowly. After about half a minute the port wheel locked into place and the indicator flickered from red to green. But the starboard wheel hung limp as the shattered wing of a bird, half-up, half-down, and the indicator stared at them red as a drop of blood.

He swore softly.

He selected "undercarriage up," expecting the wheels to retract, but they didn't move.

He selected "undercarriage down." He pulled the lever again and again; but the wheels stayed exactly where they were, the wheel to port locked firmly in place but the wheel to starboard snarled up like a flag at half mast, while the indicator glowed its warning and the sweat began to form on his forehead and roll in little salty globules into his eyes.

CHAPTER 15

"THOSE who play with fire," his daughter's voice came to him clearly above the purr of the radials, "get burned." It was, he told himself, ironic: that they should survive all the obvious hazards—the Mafia, the bends, carbon dioxide poisoning and narcosis—only to lose their lives through the recalcitrant leg of an undercarriage. Gina's fingers were tight on his arm. "The wheel! It's only half down!"

"Don't worry," he said. "We'll fix it."

She stared at him. Her eyes were enormous, but her voice was remarkably calm. "We'd better. If we want to get to that wedding!"

He was thankful she understood exactly how much was at stake.

He felt more angry than afraid. Some men would have panicked and some would have thrown up the sponge, but Peter's lips drew in with a familiar obstinacy; they were in a hell of a fix—that there was no denying—but there must, he told himself, be *some* way out.

He checked the fuel. There were a hundred and twenty-five gallons in the port tank, and a hundred and thirty in the starboard: enough to keep them airborne for nearly four hours; so at least they had plenty of time. He forced himself to try to work out logically what had gone wrong. He was sure the fault wasn't his, for he had followed the handling notes word for word; it must therefore lie in the plane. The Sea Horse's undercarriage and flaps, he remembered Blasingame telling him, were operated by hydraulics. So here was the obvious place to look for failure. He had checked the hydraulic pressure on takeoff, and it had, he remembered, been a bit on the low side (though well within the prescribed safety limits). He hadn't checked it again during the flight because he had had no occasion to draw on hydraulic fluid since setting course for Geneva. But he looked at the gauge now. And the needle hung limp on zero.

He turned to Gina. "We've a hydraulic leak."

"Is that good or bad?"

"Could be worse. We must track it down." He reached for the handling notes.

The hydraulic fluid, he found, was stored in a centrally positioned tank where the Sea Horse's wings dovetailed into her fuselage. He showed the exact position to Gina. "Could you find the tank and make sure it's full?"

While she was clambering aft to the cargo compartment, the airport controller came on the air. "Geneva Control to Sea Horse. Report position."

He did a quick check. "Hello, Geneva. Height eight thousand, fifteen miles southwest. I'm having trouble with my hydraulics."

A pause, then: "Roger, Sea Horse. Keep in touch and let us know if you need assistance."

"Thank you, Geneva. I'm not very experienced on this type of aircraft"—that, he thought wryly, was the understatement of the year!—"but I've enough fuel for more than three hours, and I'm trying to locate the trouble and put it right."

Another pause, then: "Roger, Sea Horse. We will give you all the help we can."

He didn't see how they *could* help from the ground; but it was a relief to feel that their troubles were known and to some extent shared.

The moment Gina came scrambling back to the cockpit he knew she had found something she didn't like. Her voice was breathless. "The tank's empty. There's a bullet hole in the exit pipe. And a whole lot of fluid has trickled out behind the boxes."

He cursed himself for a fool. So much had happened in the last few hours that he had forgotten the shooting of Schultz: forgotten that half a dozen bullets had whined and ricocheted about the cargo compartment. The internal organs of a plane are about as complex and sensitive as those of a human body; and one bullet, as ill-luck would have it, had lodged in a vital part. He cursed himself again for not having had the Sea Horse serviced at Luqa. But the milk was spilt too thoroughly now to be sponged away with tears. He could, looking back, identify the danger signs: the tardiness of the undercarriage to retract and the slowness of the flaps to lock into place. A more experienced pilot would have soon put two and two together. He had gone blundering on. But at least they knew now what they were up against: they had somehow to lock down the undercarriage and flaps without the use of hydraulics.

He would, given time, have arrived at the answer himself; in fact he was already thumbing through the *Handling Notes* when the voice of the controller came crackling into his earphones. "Geneva to Sea Horse. Are you having difficulty in lowering your undercarriage?"

"Hello, Geneva. Yes, I am."

"Do you have a copy of the Sea Horse *Handling Notes?*"

"Yes."

"Refer to page seventeen, section three. You should be able to lock the wheels in place by gravity."

His fingers as he flicked over the pages were clumsy with anxiety. Then as he read the instructions a great wave of thankfulness swept over him; for the wording of the *Notes* was explicit. "In the event of emergency (such as a failure in hydraulics) the landing wheels may be locked in place by selecting 'emergency down,' putting the aircraft into a controlled dive at hundred and sixty knots and pulling out at two G. Air-pressure and gravity will then combine to force the wheels into position."

He read it twice, once to himself and once to Gina. She shook her head as if it were somehow too good to be true. "So everything's all right?"

"Should be soon."

He switched to transmit. "Sea Horse to Geneva. Thanks for your help. I've read the instructions. Am climbing to ten thousand for the dive."

He headed east, over the curve of Lake Geneva. When the needle of his altimeter registered ten thousand feet he levelled off. He took a deep breath. He took a careful look below him. He smiled at Gina, crossed his fingers, selected "emergency down" and eased the Sea Horse into a careful dive. Their altimeter unwound; their airspeed snowballed, and the pressure built up fast on wings and tail. At eight thousand feet he could feel the controls beginning to stiffen; at seven thousand he could see out of the corner of his eye the struts of the undercarriage gradually straightening under the hammer-blows of the wind. Then, as at six thousand he pulled sharply out of the dive, there was a tremor, a click, and on the Sea Horse's instrument panel the light of the starboard indicator was metamorphosed from red to green.

"We've done it!"

Gina's lips moved in prayer and her fingers fell limply away from her crucifix.

"So much for the wheels!" His voice was elated. "Now for the flaps!" He climbed back to ten thousand and made, almost without thinking, the mistake that was to haunt him for the rest of his life.

He tried to lower the flaps.

It never occurred to him to doubt the wisdom of what he was doing. For he remembered the warnings that he had seen, long years ago, posted on the wall of so many wartime crew rooms: "If you think your hydraulics are damaged, test your flaps at HIGH altitude and BEFORE you come in to land." The reason for this had been simple. During the war many a shot-up bomber that had selected "flaps-down" when low on its final run-in had rolled on to its back and plunged straight into the ground, for its flaps had come down on one wing only; if, however, the flaps were tested at high altitude then the fault was discovered early while the pilot still had sufficient height to regain control.

So he selected "flaps-down." It was a mistake that no one with experience of contemporary aircraft would have made.

For perhaps ten seconds nothing happened, then the Sea Horse began very slowly to roll on to her back.

She was heavy; and she rolled like a waterlogged ship with its cargo shifting, farther and farther over. He had to heave on the control column with all his strength to prevent her toppling into a spin. He cursed, rammed open the throttles to regain speed and adjusted the trim tabs till the plane come teetering back to a more or less even keel.

"What's wrong?" The fear had come back into Gina's eyes.

"Damned flaps! They've let down one side and not the other."

"So?"

"We'll have to get 'em down both sides. Same as the under-carriage. Let's have the book of words."

It didn't come to him all at once: the terrifying *impasse* that his lack of experience had got them into. It came to him slowly: little by little, with fear building up at each successive step.

First step: there was no emergency procedure for lowering the flaps of a Sea Horse; without hydraulics it simply couldn't be done.

Second step: with one flap up and one flap down, the Sea Horse rolled on to its back the moment its speed dropped under a hundred and twenty knots.

Third step: the landing speed of a Sea Horse was eighty knots.

Conclusion: the moment they tried to land and their speed dropped, their port wing would dip into the runway and the plane, inevitably, would cartwheel on to its back.

In less than three hours they would be forced to land by shortage of fuel.

They had no parachutes.

And very little hope.

It was the thought of Gina that was almost more than he could bear. Whatever happened to him he had deserved it, and at fourty-four he had tasted most of the joys that life had to offer. But Gina . . . He felt her fingers tight on his arm. "What on earth's going on?"

"We're in trouble," he said slowly. "And I can't see a way out. Yet."

She stared at him. And gradually the fear in her eyes gave way to something that shocked him far more deeply: resignation. She looked past him and down ten thousand feet to the opposite shore of the lake. "Isn't it lovely," she said. "Look, that must be the Château de Chillon. I've never seen it before."

"Stop that!" His voice was sharp.

She blinked. For a moment she stared at him, moistening her lips. Then she tried, not very successfully, to smile. "All right. So what do we do?"

He explained with as few technicalities as possible what

had gone wrong. She was quick to cotton on to the vital point. "But those wartime bombers? How did *they* land?"

"They lowered their flaps manually. Or in some cases they sawed through the actuating gear."

"But we can't lower *ours* manually?"

"Not according to the book. We ought to have landed without flaps."

"Could we cut through the what-do-you-call-it gear?"

"We can ask Geneva." He switched to transmit. "Sea Horse to Geneva Control. My wheels are now locked down. But I'm in trouble with my flaps. The port flap is up. The starboard flap is locked half-down. And I can't move either. Have you any suggestions?"

The controller's voice was unemotional. "Roger, Sea Horse. Wait." A pause, then: "At what speed do you lose control?"

"A hundred and twenty knots."

A longer pause this time, and Peter could visualize the dismay on the controller's face as he checked the Sea Horse's landing speed; then, "We are contacting the Bolus offices in Zurich for advice. Meanwhile orbit the lake at ten thousand and experiment with trim tabs and engine settings. See if you can reduce the speed at which you lose control."

"Roger, Geneva. I have fuel for well over two hours. Will orbit the lake at ten."

He was very conscious, as the Sea Horse lost speed in her climb, of the buildup of pressure on the control column. Even at a hundred and thirty knots the plane refused to fly normally and he needed to press the stick hard over to keep her level: just *how* hard he could tell by the growing ache in his fingers and wrist. But once they had levelled off, and increased speed, she became easier to handle.

It was late afternoon now, and shadows were massing in indigo drifts in the lee of the Alps. The colours were spectacular: the virgin white of the snow, the reseda-green of the spruce and pine, the gold of alder and birch, and the occasional pool of vivid blue where little lakes lay scattered like turquoise beads across the throat of the hills. Never, he thought, had the world looked so beautiful, its every feature distilled and sharpened by his realization that he could well be looking at it for the last time.

"Don't worry," he said to Gina. "I've got out of worse trouble than this!"

They flew up and down the lake, adjusting throttles, trim tabs and controls. But the more Peter wrestled with the Sea Horse the more his dismay built up; for although he could, with full aileron tab and a touch of rudder, keep the wings more or less level at a hundred and fifteen knots, at anything slower the plane began to roll on to her back. So they would have to come in to land, he reasoned, like a bat out of hell: say at a hundred and thirty knots. This would be difficult but not impossible. The impossible came next. For the moment they touched down, their speed would automatically drop, their wing would dip into the runway, and they would be cartwheeled on to their back. And a plane that cartwheels on to its back at a hundred and twenty knots is liable to explode into little fragments tossed burning the width of the airport.

It seemed an eternity before Geneva control came back on the air. "Hello, Sea Horse. Are you ready to receive landing instructions?"

He said that he was.

"We advise that you land at one hundred and thirty-five knots, and that as soon as your wheels hit the runway you brake hard and throw your propellers into reverse pitch. We want you to try and stop as abruptly as you can, before the wing has time to drop. Do you understand these instructions?"

He repeated them back.

"Good. Stay orbiting till you have fuel for only thirty

minutes' flying. Meanwhile we are erecting a crash barrier half-way down the runway. We want you to hit this soon after touchdown to prevent a cartwheel."

For a while they talked technicalities: of wind speeds, drift angles, fire precautions and blood groups. Then there was nothing they could do but orbit: orbit and wait: orbit and wait and pray, while the fuel drained out of their tanks and the airport klaxons blared warning of emergency.

From ten thousand feet they could see the airfield quite clearly. Already it was closed to traffic; in the middle of runway two-three a crowd of engineers were erecting a net-like barrier, the fire engines were moving into position, refuelling had been halted, and in the control tower the telephones never stopped ringing. After a while it occurred to Peter that the airport police ought to be included in the alert. "Sea Horse to Geneva. Do you know what cargo we are carrying?"

"Roger, Sea Horse. We know all about your 'marine specimens.' The police and the Banque Helvétia have everything under control."

They flew up and down, midway between Jura and Alps, getting rid of their fuel.

The Sea Horse was none too easy to handle, and even with tabs fully trimmed she flew port wing low and tended to yaw off course. Peter's fingers soon grew numb, his wrist and shoulder ached and the sweat began to run cold from under his armpits. But at least he had plenty to keep him occupied, whereas Gina had nothing.

They didn't talk much. They tried to, to start with. But after a while everything they said seemed either too poignant or too trivial, so they lapsed into a silence that brought with it a sort of peace.

Nobody ever quite believes that he is going to die. The racing driver as he goes into the skid that he can't control, the matador as he feels the horn crunch into his abdomen, the doctor as he stares at the shadow on his own X ray—their first reaction is always the same: this can't be happening to me. And in Peter's case he was buoyed up by the knowledge of his skill as a pilot. He wasn't conceited about his skill; he took into account the fact that he hadn't flown for years and that he knew next to nothing of modern planes and modern techniques. But at heart he had the feeling that the issue was familiar: a damaged plane and a couple of lives in his hands. It was the sort of challenge that he had faced before, and walked away from alive. He wasn't confident, but he wasn't without hope.

It was merciful that he didn't know the feelings of the controllers in the Geneva tower. They were professionals and realists. They knew the odds. And they didn't give him a chance in ten.

There would, the controllers knew, be two moments of crisis. The first would come at touchdown. It was then, as the Sea Horse first hit the runway, that her wing would almost certainly dip into the ground and the plane would cartwheel on to her back and that would very definitely be that. It was just possible, however, for this crisis to be surmounted by a combination of luck and skill: by the pilot applying exactly the right combination or rudder, aileron, throttle and brake, and by the stabilizing effect of the wheels temporarily offsetting the difference in lift between the wings. If this happened the Sea Horse would hurtle down the runway for three or four or even (if she was lucky) for five or six seconds, losing speed rapidly, until the undercarriage collapsed. It was inevitable, the experts agreed, for the undercarriage legs to fold up under the strain of a too-fast and crablike landing followed by an emergency application of brakes. They could only hope that both legs would give way together so that the plane would slide on its belly into the safety net. If, however, only one leg gave way, then the pilot would be faced with a second crisis and would have to hold the collapsing wing off the ground for as long as he could. Every second would count at this stage: every fraction of a second. For the Sea Horse would be losing speed fast and even if she did turn over it would, now, be in slow motion. And from that sort of crash, survivors very occasionally are carried away alive.

Five o'clock. The contrails of high-flying jets streaming like multicoloured ribbons over the Alps, and the daylight fading in a riot of crimson and gold. And the voice of the controller: "Geneva to Sea Horse: report your state of fuel."

"Hello, Geneva: fifteen gallons in the port tank, twenty in the starboard."

"Roger, Sea Horse. We are ready for you whenever you want to come in."

At the moment of crisis he felt ice-cool and curiously detached. "Right, Geneva. I will make one dummy run over the airfield and will touch down at the second, repeat second attempt. Is this O.K. and understood?"

"O.K., Sea Horse. We've drinks lined up in the bar for you and your passenger. So take it easy!"

"Thanks and out."

He turned to Gina. "I want you," he said, "to strap yourself in the tail."

She shook her head. "Let me stay with you, please."

He knew that the tail, ninety-nine times out of a hundred would be safer. "Look," he said quietly, "let's not be silly about this. You'll have a better chance in the tail."

She leaned over and kissed him on the mouth. "I don't want a better chance. I want the same chance."

He thought of telling her brusquely not to be a fool, to stop acting the storybook heroine and do as she was told; and then again he thought how terrible it would be if by some freak chance the tail caught fire and he in the cockpit survived.

She took his hand. "Please, Pete. Let's see this through

together. You know what girls are today. Mad keen on togetherness!"

He didn't know what to say or do. It was a situation outside the comfortable code of rules by which he lived. "The odds are," he said slowly, "that you'd be safer in the tail. Togetherness is all very fine. But not at the risk of being killed."

She smiled. "It just so happens, Mr. Grey, that that's a risk I'm prepared to take. So you can strap me down. Here and now. Right alongside you."

He showed her the way to get maximum support from the harness. He showed her the release gear, the emergency exits, the ignition switches and the fire-extinguisher buttons. "If," he said, "we start to pile up, we switch the ignition off and the fire buttons on."

She said that she understood. And he lost height and circled the airport once at a thousand feet.

Everything was ready: the runway sprayed with foam, the crash barrier, the fire engines and the ambulances. The sun was behind the mountains now, the light was soft, and from a thousand feet the world looked homely and familiar: rows of neat little nut-brown houses, streets packed tight with cars, and toy-sized animals asleep in pocket-handkerchief fields.

"O.K. for the dummy run?"

She nodded.

He ran through the check list, gradually losing height. He took his time, then swept down in a long steady approach over the Sottens Beacon. He already knew the ideal throttle settings—with the starboard engine pulling a shade more strongly than the port to counteract the drag of the flaps—it was simply a matter of gauging the descent so that he came in over the end of the runway at a height of roughly ten to fifteen feet and a speed of exactly a hundred and thirty-five knots. He made a good run-in, noting his height over one or two salient points—a crossroads, a farm and a little cluster of trees; and the Sea Horse came hurtling over the perimeter fence at a height of under fifteen feet. He was appalled at how fast the runway went streaking under their wings; but he forced himself to let right down until the wheels were feathering the tarmac. Then, to a shattering crescendo of sound, he opened the throttles and climbed back for the final circuit.

"That was first-rate, Sea Horse"—the voice of the controller was approving. "Do it again and everything will be fine."

He looked at Gina. "O.K.?"

She smiled at him, tongue between teeth. She crossed her fingers. "Here's to our wedding."

By the time they were halfway round the circuit he had finished his checks and his prayers and the outside world had ceased to exist. One thing only existed now: the Sea Horse, the crippled incubus that he had somehow and against all the odds to hold in leash.

His second approach was as well controlled as his first. At three hundred feet he was over the crossroads; at one hundred he was over the cluster of pines, and at twenty he was coming up to the airfield perimeter.

The senior controller stubbed out the last of the cigarettes that he had been chain-smoking for the past two hours. "He's a good pilot."

The deputy controller shut his eyes. "I hope to God he's a lucky one."

He came in smooth and fast at just the right height and just the right speed. A second before his wheels brushed the tarmac he kicked off rudder to bring the plane in line with the runway. He held off, literally inches above the foam-wet tarmac, waiting for the drum-drum-thud of his wheels. It started with hardly a jar. His eyes flickered to the air-speed indicator: one hundred and thirty knots. He gave the Sea Horse a burst of throttle to keep the air flowing fast over the port wing; he eased the stick forward to keep their nose to the ground, then with a sweep of his arm he rammed the propellers into reverse pitch and hauled with all his strength on the brakes.

The force of deceleration knocked the breath out of his mouth. Instinctively, as the wing dropped, he flung over rudder and stick. The plane slewed sideways. The tires screamed, throwing out great strips of burning rubber like sparks from a wheel. And the undercarriage juddered and screeched under a strain too great to be endured, as for one, two, three, four, five seconds the Sea Horse bored down the runway in a maelstrom of smoke and foam.

"My God!" the controller's voice was high-pitched as a child's. "He's going to make it!"

Then the port undercarriage collapsed.

It was something he was prepared for but there was not much he could do about it. He slammed shut the throttles and locked the stick over hard. Already in the half-dozen seconds since touchdown, their speed had nearly halved and he knew that if he could only hold the wing off the ground for a couple of seconds more they would be safely into the barrier.

He would have done it if it hadn't been for the gold.

The wooden boxes had been lashed down securely enough for normal flight; but for the last two hours the Sea Horse had been heeled over like a listing ship, the strain on the ropes had been heavy and continuous, and one of them had worked its way to the knife-sharp edge of a box and started to fray. It had frayed slowly, almost imperceptibly, each time the plane had teetered to port. The landing had weakened it. And now the jar of the collapsing undercarriage was more than it could stand. It broke. And the boxes avalanched sideways, adding weight to the already dropping wing.

He didn't know what had happened. He only knew that at the very moment he thought they were safe, a hammerlike blow swept the control column out of his hand, and their wing tore into the ground. For a second he thought they were simply going to pivot round on the tip. Then the wing snapped off at its root. The other wing lifted, up and up, higher and higher. For a second it hung vertical, like a despairing arm upflung in supplication to the sky. Then it passed the vertical, and the Sea Horse cartwheeled in slow motion on to her back.

They saw the runway and safety barrier fall away, hang for a second at right angles and then come swinging up at them from the opposite direction. As they hit the ground inverted in a holocaust of Perspex and dural, their hands closed together over the switch of the ignition. Then they were falling through wave after wave of noise and pain into a merciful oblivion.

As he lost consciousness Peter's last thought was that Gina's hand was no longer in his. She seemed somehow, in a way that he was powerless to prevent, to be slipping away from him.

CHAPTER 16

He dreamed that he was fighting for his life in the fast-flowing River Styx.

He could recognize the familiar landmarks: the cluster of palms into whose shade his observer had dragged the unconscious Shultz, the waters dark with graphite from the hills of the Jebel el Akhdar, and the black-robed fisherman impassive in his *gaiassa* nodding away in the heat of the Libyan sun. Gina was beside him. And at first (in his dream) she struck out as strongly as he for the safety of the shore; but after a while she seemed to tire and to have difficulty in moving her arms. He caught hold of her, trying to drag her to safety. But even as he touched her he saw to his horror that her left arm had vanished and there in its place was a severed and mutilated stump. He drew back appalled, and she drifted slowly away from him, her eyes growing larger and larger and fuller and fuller with tears until they merged into the waters of the Styx and she was gone.

It was all over before he had time to realize what was happening. He heard himself cursing in impotent despair as he struck out for the spot where she had disappeared; then the water became metamorphosed to blankets and sheets and he smelt the familiar aseptic smell of a hospital ward; he was vaguely aware of running footsteps and of white-coated figures hurrying towards him. Then a needle pricked his arm and for the second time in twenty-four hours he spun down to the pit of oblivion.

He lay motionless, hour after hour and day after day, in the no-man's-land between life and death. Some of the time he realized he was in hospital; he was half-conscious of doctors and nurses, of Ken and Malloy and of a succession of half-remembered faces that he couldn't be bothered to identify; but the one face that he longed for was never there; and most of the while he thought he was back on the shore of the Blue Lagoon, watching the fisherman as he ferried a procession of familiar figures to the faraway shore: Tacchini with his wide-apart eyes, Schultz with his lantern jaw, and big Joe Blair and the maimed and ghostlike members of the Mafia. He expected any moment to see Gina step gracefully into the *gaiassa*. For in one of his rare moments of semiconsciousness he had heard a discussion which snuffed out his will to live.

There was a conference at his bedside: specialists, doctors and the nurses who had been watching him round the clock. "I can't understand it," he heard a voice saying. "He doesn't seem to be putting up a fight."

"Funny. He must know he's a millionaire."

"Do you think he knows about the girl?"

"How can he? He's never regained consciousness."

"Look! He's trying to say something."

He wanted to whisper "Gina," but he couldn't because his throat was constricted and his vocal cords wouldn't move. Cotton wool brushed gently under his eyes. "If only," one of the nurses said, "we could make him *want* to live."

That was the trouble. And he knew it. He couldn't be bothered to make the effort. It was so much easier to lie in the sun-warm sand and wait for the fisherman to row him across to the distant shore: and Gina. "Please," he kept on asking the fisherman, "please take me too." And the fisherman, as the days dragged by, seemed to be taking a more than passing interest in him.

There came a time when he was vaguely aware that he was being moved; but where to he neither knew nor cared. It didn't matter. Nothing mattered now. Except that on the Styx's sands the shadows seemed to be growing longer and darker, while the *gaiassa* moved closer inshore, and away in the distance he could hear, very faintly, the sound of music.

The music had him puzzled. What a turn-up for the books, he thought, if the heavenly choirs of the sound tracks turned out to be the real thing! But he realized after a while that it wasn't a choir whose melody came drifting over the water. It was a piano.

It would be hard to pinpoint the exact moment when he recognized Rachmaninov's Rhapsody on a Theme by Paganini.

He certainly didn't recognize it suddenly or at once. For a long time the limpid notes were nothing more than a background to the sun, the sand and the dark-flowing river. But after a while the music grew stronger and clearer, forcing itself on his attention, demanding recognition.

And it had a message.

It was a message to which he wouldn't listen at first. But gradually as the haunting melody (repeated over and over again) soaked into his consciousness a whole series of familiar vignettes began to drift through his mind like ghosts from a half-forgotten past: Anne at the piano and the French windows open and the moonlight white on the fields behind Dragonfly Cottage; Wendy floating her rubber duck in her bath, and Richard's face as he talked of the goals he had scored for his prep school's Second XI. Did the flesh of his flesh, the music whispered, mean nothing: were the joys of seventeen years to be tossed aside and forgotten: wasn't his allegiance as much to the living as to the dead?

If the piano had stopped, he would have slid back to the waters of the Styx. But it didn't stop. It went on and on, hour after hour, day after day; and all the while he was conscious of someone near him—someone who cared—willing him not to give in.

They told him afterwards that she played with hardly a break for more than sixty hours: that she wouldn't let them tape the Rhapsody and play it back because she was afraid he might know it was only a recording. He was vaguely conscious once of a voice saying, "I think he's turned the corner now." Then he slept. While the piano played on and on, bringing memories and with the memories the will to live.

The first thing he saw when he woke was her eyes looking very straight into his; the first thing he felt was her hand resting light on his shoulder. The eyes were as blue as Gina's and the hand as small and cool. But the hair that framed the oval of her face was long and gold and the mouth smiling down at him was the mouth of his daughter.

He did his best to smile back. "Hello, Anne!"

"Oh, Daddy!" she whispered. She hadn't cried in all the eleven days since the Sea Horse had crashed, but the tears came tumbling now in a flood of uncontrollable relief. And it came to him, as she clung to his hand as though she could never bring herself to let him go, that there were many faces to love.

He slept, no more than lightly drugged, for twenty-four hours.

When he woke he was still very weak but his mind was clear and he was able to talk. His daughter was sitting beside the bed, fast asleep, the afternoon sun aglint on her hair. He knew instinctively that she had saved his life and it seemed, to say the least, ungrateful that his first thought on returning to consciousness should be somebody else. But there was one thing he had to know. His hand moved slowly to hers. "Gina," he whispered.

She opened her eyes.

"Gina. What happened to Gina?"

She smiled. "Don't worry. She's all right."

He didn't believe it. If she was all right why wasn't she there beside him? "Where is she?"

"Relax, Daddy. She's been moved to another hospital."

He remembered the snatches of conversation he had half-heard between doctors and nurses; he remembered his fears as he had fought for his life in the fast-flowing River Styx: "And her arm?"

She hadn't expected him to know about that. Possible answers spun through her mind like the fragments of a kaleidoscope: a straight white lie (and he would never trust her again), an evasion (and he would spot it and imagine the worst), the truth (that, she told herself, was what he would want; she could only hope to God that he was strong enough to stand it). "Her left arm,' she said slowly, "had to be amputated. But she's out of danger. In fact the last time I saw her she was out of bed."

He shut his eyes. He made not the slightest move nor the slightest sound. It was not until she bent over him—suddenly afraid that he had lapsed back into unconsciousness—that she realized he was doing something that she had never seen him do before: not once in seventeen years. His mouth was shut very tight and tears (as if they were something to be ashamed of) were being prised in slow unwilling globules out of the corners of his eyes.

She squeezed his hand. She told him she would be back in a few minutes and walked quietly out of the room.

It was two weeks before they let him out of bed and four weeks before they agreed to let him see Gina. He had hoped, seeing that she was apparently up and about, that she might have visited him; but all he got from her was a brief and enigmatic note to say that he was not to come and see her until he was "quite fit and well." He had no intention of waiting that long. He pestered the hospital staff and worked himself into a nervous fever until reluctantly they put him in a hired car with strict instructions to the nurse in charge to bring him back in a couple of hours.

The hospital to which Gina had been moved was on the opposite side of the city overlooking the Lake of Geneva, and on the way he stopped to buy her a present. He had devoted a good deal of thought to what he should get her—the possibilities ranging from roses to an engagement ring—but in the event he spotted something in a shop window that he hoped might amuse her and bought it on the spur of the moment. He was amazed at how much it took out of him: the simple act of walking into a store and asking for something in French from a slyly amused and not very cooperative shop girl.

Ten minutes later the car was swinging in through the hospital gates.

He was trembling now, with alternate spasms of hot and cold as though in a fever, and the words that had been at the back of his mind for the past four weeks were beating *accelerando* through his mind: "There're only two things I'm *really* frightened of, being crippled and death . . . Cripples are so dependent, aren't they; such a nuisance to other people." Losing her left arm, he tried to tell himself, was less tragic than a great number of injuries that she might have suffered. But how it would affect her he didn't dare to think.

They met in the neat little visiting room, air-conditioned, scrubbed clean and smelling of disinfectant and about as romantic as a suburban café. His first reaction as she rose to meet him was one of thankfulness: she looked as attractive as ever and her arm had been amputated well below the elbow and the effect was far less disfiguring than he had feared. But the moment he kissed her he knew that things were not going to be easy. She drew away; her voice was cool and her eyes watchful. "Steady, Peter. Or you'll put up your temperature!"

He took a closer look at her, and realized that her face was too fine-drawn and that ninety-nine per cent of her colour had come from a tube.

He tried to get through to her, first by crushing her in his arms and then by words; but she was coolly evasive. Nothing he did or said made the slightest impression on the barrier of her reserve. For half an hour they sparred and talked trivialities, not much closer to one another than strangers at a cocktail party. Then, quite suddenly, he couldn't stand the charade any more. He reached for her hand. "When are we going to get married, Gina?"

She smiled politely. "I don't think," she said, "that we are."

He took a deep breath. "Now listen, please. I know that what's happened is my fault"—she tried to take away her hand but he wouldn't let her—"I know that if I'd listened to you that morning in the Phoenicia we'd be happily married now and you'd never have lost your arm. The fact that I didn't listen is something I'll never forget, and something I'll never forgive myself for. But can't we put that behind us? We were in love then; as far as I'm concerned we're in love now."

Some of the aloofness had ebbed out of her eyes, but the expression that took its place was anything but happy. "Please Peter, let's not have a scene. We're neither of us strong enough. Let's be friends."

"God damn it! I don't want to be your friend. I want to be your husband."

She took away her hand. Her fingers plucked at the hem of her sweater. "You make things difficult."

"They say the course of true love never did run smooth."

"You lawyers!" For the first time there was the faintest hint of warmth in her smile. "How you play with words!"

"I'm not playing, Gina. As you very well know."

She wouldn't look at him. "Your nurse," she said, "is outside. You shouldn't keep her waiting."

"To hell with the nurse! And the whole damned staff of the hospital. I'm not leaving this room till we've fixed the date of our wedding."

She looked at him now, very straight. "I'd hoped," she said slowly, "that you wouldn't make me say it: in words of one syllable . . . A fine wife I'd make you! I couldn't sew on your buttons. I couldn't cook you a meal without breaking half the plates. I couldn't even change your baby's nappies without dropping him on his head."

"Oh, Gina," he said, "what's happened to your courage?"

She opened her mouth, but his hand closed over hers so tightly that she quickly snapped it shut. "Please listen. I know it's easy for *me* to talk: it isn't *me* who's lost an arm. But people do wonderful things. There was a girl with one arm in the Nursing Home with Jean when she was having Richard; she had three children *and* helped her husband to run a shop. There was an English pilot in the war who lost both legs; not just one leg, both of them; he taught himself to fly and did over a hundred operational sorties. Now I don't care a damn about the buttons and plates, and I'll help with the nappies. Because I'd rather have you with no arms at all than any other woman in the world. And another thing. You ought to know by now: I may be a slow starter but I don't give up. So you needn't think that in one year or ten years or twenty years I'll change my mind."

Her eyes were full of tears. "You say it because you're sorry for me. Now. But later—" She shivered.

"Oh, Gina! You *know* it isn't true. If I wasn't so damn weak I'd carry you off to the nearest church!"

Her fingers were plucking again at the hem of her sweater. "I feel so ashamed. Like a girl who's going to have a baby!"

"What on earth do you mean?"

"I feel I've trapped you. Made you feel guilty and sorry for me. But," she looked at him defiantly, "pity's a damned poor basis for marriage."

He ran a hand through his hair. "Talk about a crazy mixed-up kid! What do I have to do to *prove* it isn't that way?"

Her eyes dropped. "Be gentle," she whispered. "And patient."

He saw how it was: he had been taking too much for granted. "I'll be gentle," he said slowly, "and as patient as I can. But you'll have to make allowances for the fact that I'm very much in love."

He half-expected her to dissolve into his arms in tears. She came into his arms all right and kissed him briefly on the mouth; but she wasn't the crying sort. The tears came later and at the moment he was least expecting them.

He was getting ready to leave when she pointed to the brown paper parcel that he had left on a table beside the window. "Don't forget your sandwiches."

"It's for you. A very silly advance wedding present."

"You're a great one, aren't you, for jumping the gun!"

"Perhaps I'd better save it." He tucked the parcel under his arm. "It doesn't seem as funny now as when I bought it."

"Now I *must* see!"

"Well—you remember that list we made: of things to take on our honeymoon?"

She nodded; and reluctantly he handed over the parcel.

After much tearing off and rustling of paper she unravelled the top half of a bikini. "Your one-track mind!" She seemed amused at first, then puzzled. She held the bikini up, then took a startled look at the box. Her eyes opened very wide. "Did *you* buy this?"

"I did. And all in French too."

She suddenly started to laugh. She laughed and laughed and laughed, on and on, hysterically, the tears astream down her face in an uncontrollable flood.

He was very considerably put out. "What the devil's the matter, Gina?"

It was some minutes before she was able to speak. "Oh, Pete! Never play James Bond again. It isn't you." She dissolved into another flood of laughter and tears. "Listen"—she at last got her voice under control—"either you're *very* unobservant, or you've given this to the wrong girl, or you expect that on our honeymoon I shall be eight months pregnant. Now which is it?"

He looked sheepishly at the box.

"Outsize," she translated for him. "Forty-four inches to forty-eight inches!"

"That damned girl. She knew very well I didn't ask for that."

She kissed him, this time as if she meant it. "Oh, Pete! Maybe you do need someone to look after you . . . Now I shall make you do a penance. Our engagement is, I think the proper word is annulled: as though it had never been. No"—she held up her hand—"please let me finish. I'm serious. Soon I shall go home to La Normanna, taking your ten million lira. You will return, a very rich man, to your children in England. Then we shall owe each other nothing: absolutely nothing. I want you to think very carefully, Peter, before you bring our paths together again."

He realized the way it was. She still thought of herself as a cripple, an encumbrance, a burden that he would have to shoulder for the rest of his life; and she was giving him the chance to be quit of her. He realized too that it would in the end be better for both of them if they made a fresh start, with the slate wiped clean of the blood, mistrust and violence of the past. "The moment I'm out of hospital," he said, "I shall bring my family south: to Brindisi."

She gave him the ghost of a smile. "Perhaps. And now you can kiss me good-bye."

The pressure of his lips would hardly have hurt the wing of a butterfly. "That very definitely," he said, "wasn't good-bye."

For the first time since he came into the prim little visiting room her eyes were neither cool nor unhappy. She squeezed his hand. "Because you are being gentle and patient," she said softly, "I will write to you. With a list of hotels in Brindisi."

EPILOGUE

THE three letters arrived within the space of a week. The first was from Ken.

Hunters' Quay,
Sarmiento,
Tierra del Fuego/Chile.
April 27th.

My dear Pete,

Congratulations! And how very kind of you to ask me to be best man. I accept; and promise not to disclose too much of your dubious past!

As luck would have it, a young chap from Bristol University has just come out to Hunters' Quay to give me a hand, so I'll be able to fly to Brindisi in good time for the wedding. What an excellent time and place to be married in—the Puglia hills are lovely in the spring—so I approve both location and bride.

You ask what I'm doing. Well, it's a long story; but basically, I suppose, we're trying to save about half a dozen tribes from extinction. The locals here are the Alacaluf. They used to number about five thousand, but now there are less than three hundred of them and their lives are unbelievably wretched. They wander about the shore in small family units, stark naked, searching for mussels which is about all they ever find to eat. There are never enough mussels, so that whole families die every year of starvation and exposure. By building a harbour and a store we hope we've given them a haven: a place they can make for in time of need. As soon as things are settled here I'm off to the islands of the south—Navarino and Hoste—where conditions and climate are said to be even worse! A lot of people might say that with the population explosion it's crazy to bother about a lot of Stone Age savages; but whenever I feel like giving up I remember the words "I was hungry and ye fed me," and the work seems very much worthwhile.

My love to Gina, and I look forward to seeing both of you soon.

Yours ever,
Ken

The second letter was from Malloy.

c/o Institute of Marine Technology,
Cordova,
Alaska/U.S.A.
April 30th.

My dear Peter,

I was delighted to hear of your forthcoming marriage, and offer you both my very warmest congratulations.

It is most kind of Signora Tacchini to invite me to the wedding. I am not entirely my own master here, but I don't imagine it will be impossible for me to find time to fly to Brindisi. I shall certainly make every effort.

You ask me what I am doing. Well, as I always hoped would happen, the publicity consequent from our salvaging the Rommel treasure stimulated a great deal of interest in underwater research. Things are moving at last. McGill have given me a degree, the Rockefeller Foundation have given me a grant, and soon I shall be off to the Aleutians to study the artificial beds of plankton that have been sown off Kiska and Attu. Isn't it an amazing thought that two million acres of this underwater plankton—an area smaller than Hawaii—could provide sufficient protein each year to satisfy the needs of the entire world! Oyster *and* Pearl *have been fitted with a mass of recording and photographic equipment, and I have every reason to believe that our underwater studies will be of the greatest value.*

I hope very much to have the pleasure of seeing you again on the 20th. With warmest regards to yourself and Gina.

Sincerely yours,
Gary Malloy

He had the comfortable feeling that things were slipping into place: like the loose ends of a well-knit novel: all neatly tied up.

But the third letter was a bombshell.

La Torre,
Siena,
Tuscana/Italy.
May 2nd.

My dear Daddy,

Congratulations! I knew you'd make it in the end!

Of course I'm not in the least upset. I must admit that when I first heard you had been sleeping with a girl from the Mafia and had given her ten million lira, I was just a teeny weeny bit alarmed! But I think Gina's an absolute sweetie, and so do Richard and Wendy; and I'm sure you'll both be blissfully happy. She has asked me, by the way, to be a bridesmaid; so mind you behave yourself at the wedding!

Now I've two other bits of news. The first will please you. But the second, oh golly, I hardly dare put pen to paper.

I've done a recording with La Scala, Milan. This is a bit unusual for a second-term student, but there are Special Circumstances (see below). It was the Rachmaninov Rhapsody. And I think I must have been O.K., because never before have so many nice old gentlemen queued up to kiss my hand! I hope the record companies are fighting madly over the rights because this will be my one and only recording.

Because—now please, Daddy, hold on to your seat and don't have a fit of apoplexy—I'm leaving Siena to get married!

His name is Carapic Hildreg; he's a student at Zagreb University reading electronics (aren't we getting a cosmopolitan family!), and twenty-one, nice-looking, and a bit square in more ways than one. And as a special concession we are postponing our wedding until you've had yours—I'm sure there's a nice legal point about a daughter not marrying before her father! Anyhow, you will see him on the 20th and if it's any consolation, Gina says you'll approve.

I've told the conservatoire I'm leaving, so there's no need for you to write. Michel Angelo was very sweet, and said that if ever my marriage busts up I could come back to Siena for free—which offer should keep Carapic up to scratch!

Have you any ideas as to what a VERY fond daughter could give her father for a wedding present?

My love to Richard and Wendy. And of course to you.

Anne

He put the letter thoughtfully into his wallet. Everything indeed had slipped into place, the loose ends were securely tied and the tapestry was complete. But the final pattern was oh so very different to that which he had imagined: woven into a design far subtler and richer than he would have dared to dream of.

He sat for a long time by the French windows staring out at the fields behind Dragonfly Cottage. The chestnuts were in flower and an old white horse, knowing that it was spring, was rolling over and over in the warmth of the sun.